CHAOS

(Horses and Souls Book Three)

Anna Rashbrook

THANKS

Dave, my husband for bearing with my determined sitting at the PC.

To Jenny, my first reader, who always puts me right!

My beta readers, Jenny Anne, Paddy, Christine and Kevin

And many thanks to the photographer Deske Wijers for letting me use the photo of Sam for the cover.

ALSO BY ANNA RASHBROOK

CONTENTS

IF YOU HAVEN'T READ COMPROMISE

Mollie and Chris met in the summer when she brought mares from the stables to visit Keith, the dippy stallion at Chris's farm. Later, Mollie needed a home after losing her job at the riding stables, being used by James, her drug addict tenant and then her dreadful parents selling her cottages. Chris needed a life free from the attention of the women from the riding club. Two friends and a deal called, 'Compromise' living.

Mollie moved in and loved the new life; milking the cows and working for Joanna, who was pregnant. However, Chris started to find that Mollie's presence upset his long-dormant sexuality; leading him to the dark side of the internet and cross-dressing. When his mother's diary was found, Chris was shocked by its revelations. He discovered he is intersex and was protected from mutilation by doctors by the intervention of the mysterious Reverend Jones. This sent him running in panic to a gay bar to meet Sandy, an internet friend.

The same evening, a seemingly repentant James talked Mollie into an apology date. On her return, she found Chris badly wounded in the barn. He had been attacked and cut badly. She, the local doctor and Sandy, treated him and, with help from the village, he recovered but only to sink into a deep depression.

It was only when badly injured Keith made a startling reappearance that Chris began to heal; the wounded becoming the healer. On the day Joanna's baby was born, her mother, Chloe, arrived and helped Chris make his peace with himself and God. James got his comeuppance on the same day when he met Chloe.

Spring. Both are free and are embarking on life without compromise. Mollie has been disowned and paid off by her parents, who never wanted her. This frees her to open a home on the farm for schoolgirls like herself, abandoned during the holidays. Chris leaves to find Reverend Jones funded by Mollie.

CHRIS

Chris drove up the steep farm track, his old truck squeaking and slipping in the mud. At last, they crested the horizon and before him, he could see the sea. Totally unlike the infringed, busy world of the Solent, the channel reaching to France. He stopped to look and take it all in and breathed a deep sigh. Rex whimpered as if it had been a long time since he had a run. Chris turned and stroked his head. 'Not far now, old boy!'

At the side of the lane, he saw the abandoned quarry that Alan had told him about; he revved up and drove in. Large blocks of Portland stone were lying around. Another vehicle was there, a very tatty Skoda, which had obviously been there a while; long grass and weeds grew all around it, and the bumper hung at an angle. He leant over and let Rex out, who leapt and rushed around the area in ecstasy; rabbits and wonderful smells.

Chris was ecstatic. The clear air was like wine. He heard the rollers on the beach, and all was good. He reached in and pulled out his backpack. It wasn't worth bothering to lock it; surely no one here would want to steal his old truck.

Giving a sharp whistle which Rex regretfully obeyed, they made their way down a steep path to the cove. They turned a corner and Chris was yet again gobsmacked at the view. All around a chocolate box beach were five small quarry workers' cottages, their white walls and stone roofs gleaming in the late afternoon sun. The hills behind seemed to hold the community in loving arms.

All seemed quiet, with no one at home; but as he looked down, a door opened, and a short plump man came out and waved. How had Alan known he had arrived? Amazing. As Chris stumbled down the path, the only thing in his head was how Alan looked completely unlike the picture in his head.

Although he had no childhood memories of him as a clergyman, he had somehow thought him tall, thin and blonde, like himself. As if it mattered. Quickly, the pair of them reached the beach and made their way over the pebbles to the first cottage. Alan waited with a grin on his face.

The two men stood and looked at each other. In those few seconds, they knew each other well. Chris sensed that this man understood his inner soul; had fought the same battles. Alan saw not only a son he would never have but also a lifelong friend; they had a lot to catch up on. He grabbed Chris's hand and pumped it up and down, beaming; even a tiny tear trying to escape.

Chris was engulfed in that loving gaze.

They would have stood there for ages, if Rex hadn't barked, demanding attention. Alan broke his grip and bent to give Rex a stoke. 'I don't know what to say! There's so much to talk about!' He looked down at the dog. 'Let's go to your cottage. Eustace is off on his travels again, so it's all yours.' Chris followed him through a blue door, and they entered the low-ceilinged cottage.

The house was open plan; a small kitchen, an immense fireplace, books on every wall, and a tatty looking sofa covered in blankets. Hidden in the corner was a steep flight of stairs. It was warm and cosy. 'It's great!' Exhausted, he sank onto the sofa.

'I think you need a cuppa!' Alan exclaimed and set about making one. Both were so unsure where to start. Soon they sat with steaming mugs and a plate of biscuits. So, of course, they both started to speak at once. After going through the 'you go firsts', Alan took over. 'Let's start right back at the beginning.'

He stroked an ever willing Rex in an absentminded manner. 'When I came to the parish of Hazeley, I was already in trouble with the church for championing a mother who had been a victim of domestic abuse. They told me I should have handed the case over to social services much earlier, but she wouldn't have it. I met your parents quite soon afterwards. They were keen church members, although your mum was huge with you. You told me you have read her diary. I don't need

5

to repeat all that. I was on a duty hospital visit shortly after those cursed, big-headed doctors had been in.

They wanted to mutilate you into the gender they thought you were – DNA analysis was in its infancy then. They planned operations and hormone treatments, all to correct something that didn't need treating. Never a thought about counselling or support for you or your parents. I fought for you and in the process lost my parish, ending up in an admin job. I never regretted it for a minute, as I saved you from them. As I had been the victim of such ministrations, I would not let you be the same.' Chris knew this story, but guessed that Alan had to work his way through it.

I was born a girl, as my parents wanted and prayed for, but they gave in to the doctors and I spent time in hospitals, operations and had various hormone treatments until I rebelled and became what I wanted to be. I chose to present as a man. My vocation was to be a vicar. There were no women in ordination then. I've got used to the clothes. I don't feel like anything except me.'

Chris sat up. 'That's what I want to be, but how do I do it?'

'Well, you don't have the problem of wanting to change, just be you. You mustn't worry about what people see. We've both discussed this so much in the emails. I think it's time for you to move on.'

'How do you mean?' This response wasn't

what Chris had been expecting.

'Stop obsessing about your gender. You don't need any tests or hospitals.'

Chris grimaced. 'I can't function as a man; there was precious little there before and now nothing.' His voice rose with some anger.

'Stop thinking about it. You're in a place of peace. Meet the others tonight. This is a haven of real healing. You need to sort your soul out and the body needs to take second place for a while.' Chris's feathers were ruffled. He had expected quick answers.

Alan was grinning at him. 'Don't get antsy, I've been in your place. There is love in plenty for all, but most of all you must rest. No cows, no farm, no Mollie, only you and Jesus. Trust me.' In that smile, Chris was suddenly all-encompassing and unconditionally safe, something he had never found in a person before. He saw they had eaten their way through the pile of biscuits without noticing, and he was still hungry. 'Do I need to stock up?'

'There's lots of basics in the cupboards, and dog food under the sink. We'll all eat later with Sam; she's done her famous cottage pie in your honour. Let me take Rex for a run in the fields, while you unpack that huge bag. You left the laptop behind as I said?' Chris nodded. Alan leapt up and was out with Rex in a trice, leaving Chris bemused on the sofa. What had he expected?

As he thought he realised he had been

looking for a home and an end to the dilemmas that kept on wracking him, he had been relying that Alan would hand it all to him on a plate, and there would be an instant solution. He clambered up the narrow stairs and found a small bedroom with an even smaller shower room. It was easy to throw his stuff in a cupboard and put his Bible beside the bed.

He lay on the bed, which was so soft and comfortable that he wanted to doze off. Chris forced himself up. Back in the sitting room, he saw there was no TV, he saw some sockets. It seemed there had been deep planning for his arrival. They had him sussed. He smiled, sensing it was okay. He looked at his watch and wondered how long it was until food? A soaked Rex came bounding into the cottage and shook himself leaving splashes up the wall. In a panic, Chris looked for a cloth, but Alan popped his head around the door.

'Don't worry about that, Eustace has a dog, well, he calls it one. Grubs up, we eat early here, come on!'

Chris followed Alan along the narrow path to the cottage at the end. He ducked under the now familiar low door and was met with a blast of cottage pie steam. Inside stood two women grinning as if there was a joke they had shared, and then they burst into laughter as they looked at Chris. He stopped in astonishment, Alan bumping into him. Chris found himself engulfed in a double hug that reminded him of Chloe.

'Forgive us! It's just Alan has said so much about you that we had this picture of you in our heads and we were both wrong. She had you as this big bronzed, farming hunk with a straw in your mouth.' The older woman winked at the younger. 'And I had you still in short trousers and school uniform! Oh, dear, do forgive!'

Chris was totally taken aback, it reminded him of two of the women at the local riding club who had pursued him for a few years. He forced a smile. 'So, am I worse or better?'

'Better,' He forgave them and found himself being propelled into a seat. Rex was now getting the smothering. Chris sighed in relief and looked across to see Alan grinning at him again.

'They do improve, I promise!'

After Grace, the pie was swiftly served with a large glass of wine, and there wasn't much more than general conversation until they had cleared the plates. It took two helpings for Chris to feel replete. He watched Rex cleaning his bowl in the corner.

'Right now, proper introductions,' said the older woman. 'My name is Sam; I've been here for five years. I used to be a primary school teacher before I retired. My two children are somewhere backpacking around the world. My time is filled with writing, painting and making a nuisance of myself in the local church!' She was certainly something to look at, her hennaed hair was wound in a coil around her head, and she wore a very hippie, floating blue dress.

'I'm June, I've been here a year. I work in Swanage in a gift shop and before that I was a drug addict. Well, some say I still am, but I'm here thinking what to do next.' She was in simpler jeans and t-shirt, but she also had very long, blonde hair that cascaded down her back. Chris couldn't quite place what it reminded him of. They didn't seem to expect him to reply, and it appeared they knew all about him, which was both disquieting and a relief.

Alan took over. 'We're a close little community here. Eustace, who owns the estate all around here, restored the first cottage a few years ago and afterwards built more for guests. You can't tell which one is the original one anymore where they're so well built. People he meets come here and stay for a while, then move on. I've been here the longest. He's been talking about charging me rent. We're all Christians, as I told you, and we try to be like it was in the early days; we share, we love and help each other, spiritually, financially, or any way that is needed. The Bible is our rule book.'

That all seemed fine to Chris. Since he had made his peace with God and re-taken Jesus into his life, he had been reading the Bible and praying in a gentle way that seemed to percolate through his body. Few questions were answered yet, but Alan told him clearly that there weren't going to be any quick fixes. Chris, overwhelmed with the peace, yawned; tiredness engulfed him.

'Looks like the Purbeck air is having its effect; you seem all in! Leave your front door on the latch and if you sleep in, I'll take Rex for a walk in the morning,' offered Alan. Chris didn't have the energy to say Rex was a farm dog and never expected to go for a walk, so he nodded and smiled. He made his way out into the gloom to a chorus of goodnight wishes. Around him, he heard strange sea birds calling in the night, and in the distance, he almost felt the throb of a boat's engine. The cottage was warm, the underfloor heating taking care of that, it wasn't so primitive. Chris threw himself into bed and fell into the deepest slumber he had had for years.

He awoke to the sound of a dog barking from the direction of the beach and blearily looked at his watch. He shot up in horror when he saw it was the middle of the afternoon. No guilt, no milking, no cows, no Mollie with another hairbrained scheme. No stupid stallion bellyaching that the mares weren't paying him any attention. That's it. June's hair was exactly the same colour as Keith's flowing mane and tail. He smiled to himself. Complete freedom. No ties. No farm. No one looking at him with that odd, inquisitive look. All the negatives were positives.

Even though the village had known his problems, and had accepted him none the less, he was still other. Here they had all the details, but he was one with them. Last night had been the one time in his life when he had a sense of complete

11

acceptance by people around him. It had been right to flee the farm.

He sat up and stretched. He'd never realised how deep-seated his tiredness was. Now it had vanished for the first time in years. He had awoken refreshed, not burdened. He started to dress and saw he had packed and prepared badly, too few clothes; it was daft to think he could leave with a rucksack... he would ring Mollie. No, he wouldn't came the simultaneous reaction. He would pop into Swanage or Weymouth and buy new. Mollie's financial support meant no problems with shopping and outings in reasonable limits. Had he had been subconsciously trying to leave his past behind when he took so little? Chris smiled in the mirror at himself, called himself a prat, and got dressed.

Alan must have left a long cold cup of tea for him, but he drank it anyway. Rex must be having the time of his life on the beach. For early spring, he found the weather wonderfully mild as he opened the door. He brewed a fresh pot of tea and sat on the bench in the weak sunshine. Glorious, why hadn't he done this before? He'd seen Mollie do it enough, and he'd never joined in he had too much work. Not now though. He stretched and his knuckles cracked.

'I wouldn't do that too often. Air in the joints isn't good for you!'

Chris jumped out of his skin. June stood beside him casting a cooling shadow. She sat down beside him.

'I've got a day off today; I work at the stables on the estate. Alan said you used to have a stud on your farm. Was it New Forest ponies?' Trying not to be grumpy, he formed an answer. The pain from his scars meant riding was painful. That grieved him more than all the other injuries.

'No, it was only working cobs. I've still got two broodmares and a daft Welsh stallion who has a harem on the hills in the summer. I don't ride anymore,' he said firmly.

'Ah... I'm popping into Swanage for some shopping. Would you like to come?'

'How do you get there? I was told no one has cars and to leave mine at the top,' asked Chris.

'That's only to stop the bolters from running. Some people arrive and can't handle things, but the walk up that path is a hard one, and it makes people stop, think and consider; then mostly they stay.'

'Bolters?'

'Eustace is always finding people who need help. He drags them here and they either get better or run away. It's only us hard cases that want to stay!'

'Do I look like a bolter?'

'No, you ate the cottage pie last night and didn't notice that she hadn't put any real meat in it. You'll stay.' Perplexed, Chris laughed with her. 'I haven't had breakfast yet, but I do need some shopping. Yes, I'd like to come. What shall I do about the dog?'

'Simply leave a note on Alan's door. He's in seventh heaven. He's been on and on about a dog, but Eustace's spaniel can be aggressive. Now Rex is here, something will change, I'm sure. We can have fish and chips or an all-day breakfast if you want. Let's go.'

Caught up in another feminine whirlwind, Chris got his wallet and followed her around the back of the cottages, where he found an old mini parked in the small lane. They bumped and rolled up the pothole filled hill; the mini scraping itself wherever possible.

Eventually, they hit tarmac. June drove like a rally driver, but also waving her hands and pointing as they passed the main house and the stables. To his relief, once on the main road, she put her hands back on the wheel. They talked their way along the road.

'I say I'm not a drug addict, not like the people who go to AA and DA meetings because I am healed. I was prayed over so many times that I know I'm okay. All that didn't work before is now in order again.'

'Are you giving me some subtle hints?' Chris smiled.

'Yup, whatever your problems are, you have the power within to release the healing, or we'll all pray for you. It's all quite simple.' No, it's not, Chris thought, but he said nothing.

'Take your time and chat with us all. When

you hear Sam's story, I think you'll get it. Look, I've taken the old road, let's play spot Corfe Castle.'

Within a few minutes, they saw the ruin in the distance, like something from a fairy tale, but it flew quickly out of sight. They turned and found themselves surprisingly right at the foot of its ruins. Chris gawped up at its ruined silhouette. They drove through the grey stoned village; which even for this early in the year, was full of visitors.

'The emits never stop. Did you know that's Cornish dialect for ants?' June laughed. She swung up a steep hill where they saw the coast and Corfe from another side. It was Chris's first time in this part of the world, so he let the beauty of the landscape wash over him.

The walled fields, bent trees and the sweeping ocean were glowing in the weak sun. The car soon swept down into the town of Swanage and June parked near the railway station. Chris had forgotten the steam trains and watched in fascination as one puffed away.

'I thought you were hungry?' That worked. Chris was propelled by a determined June past interesting shops to a fish bar that looked over the seafront. The waves hit on the quay walls, and a seagull sat on a light fitting, watching them through the window with great interest. Before Chris could do any more than wonder if it was a herring gull, a heaving plate of chips and battered cod was set in front of him.

'Go on farm boy, get yourself around that!' Chris choked at the term but chose to obey. In the short time he'd met June, he was bowled over. Mollie seemed quiet and retiring in comparison. As he munched came the sudden realisation, he had been doing nothing with his life; he'd never walked around a seaside town or even eaten fish and chips. There had been precious few holidays with his parents. Had it been the overprotectedness or simply lack of time? The answers were lost forever. At least June was quiet while she ate.

'That was amazing! Thanks,' said Chris as he poured the last cup of tea. She smiled. 'Now shopping, what sort of stuff do you need?'

'Only some clothes, bits and pieces.'

'There's a big supermarket by the station with a clothes department, and various more expensive ones along the Highstreet. Meet you back at there in a couple of hours?' She rushed off, swinging her mane and leaving him with the bill.

Chris was relieved to be left alone. This wasn't at all what he had expected. He had thought it would be long deep talks with Alan, and now he had landed in another world.

In the next couple of hours, he found a new joy. Browsing in charity shops, buying treats for Rex in the pet shop, second-hand books to read, laughing at the t-shirts in the hippie shop and buying cakes and goodies to take back with him. He even remembered the clothes. It was with regret he walked up the Highstreet to meet June at the station. He had more bags than he could easily carry.

'Got slightly carried away with yourself?' she grinned.

Chris knew he was blushing, but bundled the goods into the boot. He had to come here again. On his own; to mooch some more. He'd never had such a pleasant afternoon. What had he been doing with his life?

'I'll drop you off, then I'm off to Wareham to see a friend, that OK?' June had been telling him about the shops he'd missed but he had only been half listening. After the bouncing down the lane, he was unloaded. She tore away again in a cloud of smoke from the overworked mini. Rex was lying in a heap and barely opened an eye as he entered; totally knackered from his adventures with Alan.

Chris spent a happy time unpacking and gloating over his goodies. Shopping had been fun, but he probably shouldn't get hooked on it. He made himself a snack and sat once again in the sunshine to eat it; Rex managing to force himself to help with the crusts. It was so good to sit and not do anything.

His mind filled with empty, shallow thoughts. No having to worry or analyse anything at all. The waves had a therapy of their own. He fetched his book on the Purbecks and Bible, then enjoyed a blissful couple of hours dipping in and out of both. It was an enjoyment he realised with a start that came from not having to check his watch constantly for milking. He was utterly at peace. The sun began to dip down behind the hills and it quickly got cold. Alan was cooking, so man and dog sauntered over.

Opening the door, the rich smell of steak and onions greeted them. Alan's flat was a revelation. Chris had never seen so many books, floor to wall, stacked in heaps, in boxes and shelves. Besides a huge TV was a couch that begged you to sit on it and read all of those books while you enjoyed the fire. Alan stood at the stove. 'Had a good day?' He swung around and Chris couldn't keep in the gasp. Alan had make up on and was wearing a smock like garment, with a rampant flower design.

'You trying to tell me something?'

'Simply showing you what you can be if you want. I only do this sometimes these days. I can't be bothered so much now.'

'I tried, but it seemed wrong.'

'But you weren't yourself then. It was before your attack; you've moved on from that point. You may see things differently now. Here you can experiment in peace.' That word again. Alan looked a little like a clown to Chris, and he found that quite unsettling. He had been admiring Alan for all his advice and shared experiences; now it seemed he wasn't the star he had imagined.

Whatever. But he so wanted for this to stay perfect. For it to fill his need for a new start with no mistakes; a new ground to rebuild from. No faults. Trying to hide his discomfort, Chris went to the books.

'I found a great second-hand bookshop in Swanage today. I could have spent a fortune there!'

'What did you buy?'

Alan came over and Chris found the closeness now disturbing.

'I've got a history of the coast here. There are lots of great photos in it!' He showed Alan the book, and they turned a few pages together.

'There are loads on the Purbecks over there by the fridge. Borrow as many as you want. This wall is all my Christian section; there are my novels, and in the corner, my what I call dodgy books!'

Chris looked askance.

'Well, I started with Oscar Wilde, followed by Virginia Woolf and I'm now onto people like Madeline Miller.'

'Why do you need to keep them in a separate place?' Chris knew nothing about books but was starting to think for himself. Why should they be separate? Alan turned to face him.

'That's quite a question! I've never thought about that, it sort of happened. If I'm to be honest, there might have been a bit of shame there; wanting to keep separate. Let me think about this?' He grinned. 'Looks like we're going to learn from each other!!'

He was saved by the bell as Sam and June came bursting in. Once again, a pleasant evening passed as they all began to understand each other a little better. Chris found it easy to begin opening up. He told them about the farm and the horses he'd owned. The thrill of the foals and breaking them in the cows and how they weren't numbers but names with personality.

Then, in the same breath, he had to admit how much he was enjoying not milking. He had told no one else all of this and was surprised at their genuine interest. Sam even asked to come and visit when he returned home. Before long, he yawned and blamed it on the sea air. Another night of deep, untroubled sleep followed.

A thundering on the door had him sitting up in a panic. Alan was yelling up the stairs. 'Chris, we've got a problem. Can you come down?'

Rex rushed out and Chris, in milking mode, threw his clothes on, and he stumbled down the steep stairs. Alan and Sam hovered by the sofa; Alan with a piece of paper in his hands, which he thrust to Chris without a word.

Dear All,
It's time for me to move on. I have found a new job
and somewhere to live. I've been waiting on Chris's

arrival and now he can take over the stables for me. I've written a list and messaged Kathy to tell her, so all is ready for this week.

Thanks so much for your love and healing. I am a new person; my identity in Christ is secure and I know I won't backslide. I am going to treasure my memories of you all, and perhaps I will pop back soon, and we can catch up.

June

Chris felt like he was being dowsed in a shower of iced water. He sat down without a word, only aware of a huge overwhelming rage that he had never experienced before rising in him.

'No.' As he spoke, the anger came out. 'I will not do this. It's not what I came here for, and you all know that. I've had enough of being tied to flipping animals. This is my chance to break away and begin afresh. I AM NOT GOING TO DO IT! Were you all part of the plan, too? Find a mug to come along and dupe into working here?' His voice finished on a shriek. Alan laid a placating arm on him, but Chris shook it away.

'Get off me, don't you dare touch me!' Where did all that come from flitted through his mind?

'Chris, calm down!' Sam now intervened as a speechless Alan backed off. Her voice was somehow deeper and stronger than before, and it stopped him in his tracks. 'We're not asking you to! We need you to come with us to the yard this morning and help us get it sorted out. Calm down. We are just as annoyed as you are. She's left the flat a tip…oh, and please don't flip again, we suspect she might have taken your truck; the mini is still here.'

Chris took flight and ran up the cliff path, rage fuelling his speed. At the crest, his heart was pounding and his legs weak. He didn't need to go further; he could see it was indeed gone. Gasping for breath, he sank to the ground. Rex came bounding up, thinking it some new game.

For a split second, Chris wanted to shove the slobbering beast back down the cliff. But of course, he wouldn't and in remorse hugged the bewildered dog to him, 'You, stupid dog, can't you leave me alone for five flaming minutes?' His sanity returned as his face with Rex's frantic face washing. He would now have to make his apologies, and he didn't want to. He was still angry with them, even though they weren't guilty. Everything seemed a trap, and he was suffocating inside. Nevertheless, he came more slowly down to where they sat on the bench. They waited for him to speak.

'It's gone. How she found out that you can start it under the dashboard I don't know, I never told her. It wasn't locked. It has about a week's MOT on it. Oil is leaking from the sump, and the battery is on its way out. Serves her right.'

'Will you report it?' asked Sam.

'Half of me says yes, she can't be far away.

The other says let her get nicked or have to pay for the repairs.' The anger seemed to have seeped away, but he wasn't going to say sorry yet. 'I suppose we have to make sure the horses are okay.' He couldn't escape from his deeply ingrained sense of responsibility for animals. In silence, they piled in the mini and drove at a decorous speed up the lane; this time avoiding the potholes.

'We've rung Eustace on his emergency number. We don't know what time zone he is on, so an answer might be a long time in coming.'

'He'll employ someone to take over?'

'I should think so, but it may take a while to get them.' Chris sensed that ball of fury rising inside again. He squashed it like he was already squashed on the backseat of the mini. They turned a corner into the stable yard. Their piling out of the car started a cacophony of neighing and banging of stable doors. Chris had to take control, as the others were looking completely hopeless.

'Where's the feed room?'

Alan seemed to pull himself together. 'This way.' Inside they found piled up prepared feed bowls. Fortunately, names were written on the sides, so Chris divided them out. The noise got worse. He saw Sam and Alan looked quite worried. 'Follow me. I guess you don't want to be flattened!'

As he went to the first stable, the pinkest, most whiskery nose he had ever met nearly knocked him out and then it yelled in his face. The nameplate said Doris, and Sam handed him the correct bowl.

Giving out a roar, he opened the door and shoved, but the face only wanted the bowl and shoved back, so he slid it through the gap and slammed it shut. Next door was no better; the horses were starving. Thankfully, as they took the bowls down the line, silence and munching followed.

Chris heaved a sigh of relief and smiled. 'So, I guess at least she did her bit. But she had a day off yesterday. Who looked after them?'

'I've no idea, but it might be worth pursuing. What needs doing next?' Alan read June's list. Chris, despite himself, walked along the boxes and looked inside. After the enormous piebald Doris, was a smaller piebald, Harry, then another, then another. All piebald, variously sized, heavily rugged and clipped. His heart sank, why make so much work when they could all be out, after all, they were just cobs? When he got to the last door, something made him look again, because he recognised the markings on the mane. A distinctive stripe halfway down. It was one of the horses his dad had bred. Sadness tugged at him.

A car swung into the stable yard and a tall blonde woman emerged in a rush, a deep frown on her face. 'I thought I must come early when I got June's message. Typical of her to take off and leave us all in the dung!' She swung a hand at Alan.

'I'm afraid it's all a bit of chaos. I don't know the first thing about horses, nor does Sam, but Chris used to have a stud and arrived here a few days ago,' he said.

'I guess she simply expected him to want to be in charge?'

'You've got it.' As if dismissing Alan, she now strode over to Chris and he found his hand being mangled. 'And will you?' she demanded. A laser like stare fixated Chris, but his anger, so neatly bottled up, saved him.

'Absolutely not. I have come here for a break and no way am I getting involved.' He glared back.

Kathy returned the glare in a battle of wills, but Chris won. She sighed. 'But would you help me just for today? The Swanage school will be here in an hour and we must be ready.'

'Ready for what?' He held onto the anger.

'Did she not explain? We're a Riding for the Disabled centre. I'm a physiotherapist, so I run the sessions. Before long, about six helpers will arrive, followed by minibuses, wheelchairs and kids who need help.' Ah, she was trying the soft soap. 'June usually gets the horses groomed and tacked up. The helpers then take them according to the session and we get the kids on board. They either do some simple activities or therapy work.'

Chris took in a strange ramp at the side of an arena, a hoist, and heaps of containers filled with toys. 'June was invaluable as she keeps an eye on the volunteers as they sometimes tack up and she gets the special equipment ready. Without her, this morning will be chaos; we have all four sessions booked. Would you help today, so we don't let anyone down? Sue, the most experienced helper can show you where things are.' She made the Bambi eyes at him. Out of the corner of his eye, Chris saw the other two heading slowly towards the mini. He was completely trapped.

'Today only and that's all,' he said brusquely, seeing his trip back to Swanage disappear to the muck heap. 'Where's the tack room?' He found his mangled hand being pumped again, and he was dragged away. It was in perfect order. For all of June's sins, she had kept a good yard.

'Why don't the helpers do the tacking up and grooming, and this Sue?'

'Some of them aren't that horsey; they're more into the kids. Others won't and some will but don't have a clue, despite the best intentions. We need to press on. At best, can you get me Doris and Amigo with saddles and bridles ready for the first session? After that, I need Spot in the vaulting equipment for the second. I've got two of the better helpers with Sue here this morning. They understand what the sessions require.' Chris shrugged and went along with it; he had no choice.

Doris had calmed now she had eaten breakfast. She stood quietly as he took the rugs off and groomed. He cursed to himself as he saw she had trashed her box. It would need a major muck out. At least he had wellies on, he hadn't even noticed putting them on in the rush. The dreaded helpers must do some work. Why on earth were the horses on deep straw when underneath was rubber matting? It would be so much easier with shavings.

He shook himself as he realised what he was thinking. Oh, no, he wasn't going to get sucked in. He had Amigo quickly ready too; just as the first helpers began to arrive. To his relief, Kathy took over and bossed them, too. They were putting toys and cones out in the school as he watched over the stable door, keeping well out of the way. Soon two middle-aged women in hard hats, gripping leading reins, bore down on him. He got Doris out first.

'You've forgotten the neckband, and these are the wrong stirrups!' she barked.

'Shut up Jenny, he's new here. I'll get them.' The first woman took Doris and removed the stirrups from the saddle. 'We use extra short leathers for this group as they're all under ten. They'll have to be changed back later, though.' The stirrups were soon replaced, and they led Doris away. He sneaked in and changed Amigos before the next lot of bullies arrived. Chris was looking at the vaulting equipment feeling completely perplexed when a younger woman came in.

'I'm Sue. Let's get the vaulting equipment, is Spot clean?' At least she was smiling.

'Not yet, but if you bring the gear, I'll soon sort him.'

Spot was small, about 13 hands, but even

so, had also made a mess in the box. Chris tied him on the yard; perhaps the rugs were a good idea after all, as he only had a yellow mark on his one white leg. Sue returned, barely visible under the tack, so he took some of it and put it on the stable door. He watched Sue work. She seemed much younger than he had thought, with severely cropped black hair which accentuated her big eyes.

The bridle had a thick noseband on with rings and extra buckles on, fitted far tighter than he would have liked. Then a huge blanket like thing made of soft rubber was thrown over his back. After that a surcingle, but with two leather loops that looked like places to hang on. Sue gave him two rolled up bandages, that was easy to do. Spot looked most odd by the time Chris finished.

A minibus had arrived and parked near the ramp. Chris was surprised to see two wheelchairs being taken up the ramps. How would these go on the horses? They led the two horses up to the ramp. With a teamwork that spoke of familiarity, the helpers rolled the wheelchairs onto the ramp and with ease shifted the kids straight on to the horses. Another helper stood on the far side keeping them safe.

The two wobbly kids, dwarfed by their riding hats, sat up. They took the reins and were led away. Even at this distance, Chris saw the big grins on their faces. Forgetting he should be mucking out, Chris watched them play games with bean bags, hug the horses and even have a go at guiding. It seemed the lesson was over too soon for them as one burst into tears when the wheelchair returned. Protests ignored; they were both bundled away.

Engrossed, Chris watched the second group too. The five of them were more able and full of noise. They jumped about, all dressed in matching tracksuits. Spot started to work on the lunge line in a wide circle. Kathy raised her arm and one of the kids ran in and stood behind her. When she lifted her arm again, he ran in to walk beside Spot. They did this until all marched with him at a shoulder or hip; Chris saw them coordinating their steps with the horse. After this, they all filed out but then took turns on Spot. They legged each other up to sit behind the surcingle, they swung legs, turned around, one even stood up arms stretched out wide.

'Are we going to put the horses back into dirty boxes or will you muck out?' It was that woman again.

'Sorry,' muttered Chris and went to find the tools. Halfway across the yard he stopped and turned, fuelled with that sudden anger. 'I don't know who you are, or what you understand I am doing here, but I am not a slave. I am not employed here or anything to do with this set up. You can stop bullying me, get the tack and muck the stables out yourself. All right?' He squared up to her, and she seemed to shrink.

'I apologise, I thought you had taken over

from June.'

'No, I haven't, and even if I had, you have no right to speak to anyone like that!'

He turned on his heels leaving her looking aghast. He was chuffed that for the first time in his life that he had actually stood up to someone; where had that all come from? He felt feet taller as he strode off and got mucking out. He shifted the worst of the unnecessary bedding, leaving the clear. That woman gave him a glare when she brought Doris in but kept her peace. Chris refilled the hay nets, left the horses munching and watched the session. The kids were all now on the horse at once and trying not to laugh. Soon they finished, and yet another minibus pulled in.

This time one wheelchair was taken out, in it a very limp body dressed in pink, lay with arms akimbo. There came a sort of visceral grunting coming from him or her. He looked closely as she passed. A peculiarly shaped head, eyes close together and dribble running down the chin. It revolted Chris but had enough respect to turn away.

He both did and didn't want to look; he kept his eyes on the horses. Such disability he had never seen before. Was this girl a vegetable or was there a trapped person inside? Either possibility had his stomach churning. That nasty, sneaky voice that he had fought for so long after the attack returned started up. You are like her; you just carry your damage on the inside. He wanted to throw up and slunk around the stables away from the action.

Chris leant against the wall breathing deeply. This wasn't what he had come to find. Where were the deep conversations with Alan and finding more about himself? Only yesterday he had been swanning about Swanage, eating fish and chips. Finding a new part of life which he desired so much to explore? He had to leave; the helpers should finish the stable work. Not his problem. Without meaning to do so, he looked at the arena. They gently moved the girl onto Spot. He now had a huge blanket over his back. She lay on her back with someone at each corner. The grunting had become high pitched and in rhythm with the horse's hoofbeat. Still not good, he had to go. He swung to the lane and escape.

'Hi, Chris, would you give us a hand with the lunchtime feeds?' That woman smiled a winsome, friendly smile that he had seen so often before. The one that was designed to win a male over. A huge cloud rained on his anger. 'I'll show you, but then I must go.' She followed him into the feed room where he demonstrated to her how measure to and fill the scoops and where the diets written on the wall along over the named buckets.

'It's not rocket science, make sure all are damped down with some water.' He finished.

'June used to have it everything ready for us.'

'Well, I'm clearly not June and I'm not

staying!'

'Why not?'

'I am here on a holiday. I'm not taking over the yard. I've walked away from animal work to make a new start.'

'Oh, I understand.' She said unbelievingly and stalked out with feed buckets.

Kathy walked in. 'Thanks, so much for your help this morning, I'm sorry if Mrs Trotter is a little full on. She's nervous underneath and is hiding it.'

'It's not my problem, I'm not taking over.'

'But what am I supposed to do? I have bookings all this week.' Chris noted the tears starting to well, not going to work.

'I don't see why your volunteers can't do it until someone is found. The whole system here is set up to be working intensive, when with a bit of organising, it should be easy.'

Kathy looked puzzled.

'None of these horses need to be in. They're all cobs. If you're worried about them being dirty, I've seen New Zealand rugs with neck guards on them. Then you can turn them out.

The stables all have rubber matting, I can't understand why they are on straw. If they only come in for work, then all that is needed is to put some shavings down and keep them skipped out. The whole lot are overfed. I'm surprised you haven't had them taking off. You can show your helpers how to tack up, although they all seem to know pretty well after that they can learn how to clean tack and keep it in order. Is there a turn out field?'

'Yes, a huge one, about twenty acres. It's off the yard. But you must understand, we must keep up to British Horse Society standards for our licencing and for the RDA inspections. We need qualified stable staff.'

'Rats to them, in that case, why me? I never even took the pony club tests,' answered Chris bluntly. 'This will keep you ticking over until this Eustace employs someone. What about this Sue? She seems on the ball?'

Kathy sighed, 'She's only 17, I can't leave her in charge. I suppose I don't have any choice. Will you come back later to check everything and help turn out?'

Chris heart sank again, but he had to be fair. 'What time do you want me?'

Rex came bounding out of the cottage as Chris opened the door, he had forgotten all about him. Rex rushed off to the last one, so Chris followed. Inside was a picture of chaos. Alan and Sam were bundling up rubbish into plastic bags.

'I can't believe she left this place such a pigsty, why didn't she take all these clothes with her?'

'We'll take them back to the charity shop

where she probably got them!' said Sam. 'Hi Chris, did you get the stables sorted out?'

'I've made it clear I'm not stepping in. But I am going back later to show them how to turn the horses out and leave the boxes ready.'

'That's kind of you. Eustace has sent a message to say he has put the position in the local and national job centres, so hopefully, the problem won't last long.'

'That's a relief. This is a bit of a contrast to how she kept those stables. She made work for herself there. The horses are overfed and spoilt.'

'I think she made them her family, hers threw her out. Would you help us with these bags? Did you report your truck?' asked Alan. Chris had forgotten all about it. 'I guess I have to, or I'll be nicked if there's an accident.' He reached for his phone, then remembered he hadn't got one anymore. 'Use this landline,' smiled Alan. Once the formalities were done, Chris helped with the bagging up of stuff. Slowly the rooms re-appeared. 'Doesn't anyone check on each other, or pop in and out?'

'No, she kept her door shut, and we respected that. Would you like to move in here, then Eustace's place is ready if he returns?'

'No problem, I've not got much.' He did the move swiftly and soon settled in. It surprised Chris how he found this more relaxing. The other cottage although identical was another person's home. They all sat and ate sandwiches; Rex assisting.

'This is more of what I was expecting,' said a full Chris.

'What was that exactly?' asked Sam.

'Some space to find me. As you know, I've worked all my life on the farm. Going into Swanage had me see that I've never spent time knocking about, exploring, trying new things. Not being tied to routines. I want to explore what I believe and who I am.'

'So, even in a couple of days, you've stopped stressing about your gender?' asked Alan

'It hadn't crossed my mind.' But he heard that voice in his head again. 'I will not get bound to that yard, and I will stand up to those women!' The anger welled again.

'Good for you!' grinned Alan. 'Tonight, we usually have some time together Bible reading and discussion, will you join us? I'm cooking!'

'Just what I want. About cooking, I'm rubbish at it. Maybe on my night we could get a takeaway or go for a pub meal on me?' The other two grinned and agreed on the deal.

Chris and Rex made their way up the hill to the stables, enjoying a slightly cool breeze. The rolling Purbeck hills were beautiful, and the sense of the sea was a balm. He could hear again the drone of a fishing boat. The stable yard was quiet, the

horses occupied with haynets. Chris was relieved the clients had finished for the day.

He looked over in the stables and saw all the now naked horses were still on matting although they hadn't been skipped out. He found Sue, Kathy and Mrs Trotter having a cuppa in the tack room. Everything looked in order and hung up.

'Looks like you don't need me after all!' They all jumped.

'Well, we do, we have looked at those rugs and need help putting them on,' said Mrs Trotter.

'Right, let's get them and crack on!' He got the rugs from the small room behind the feed room where they hung above a dryer.

'You seem well set up here, these rugs can take days to dry out...oh, and they're named. Brilliant. Let's pop them over the stable doors with the head collars and do one together.' Hey, this bossing people about wasn't bad. Even Mrs Trotter almost smiled and didn't argue.

They hauled Doris out, and Chris demonstrated to them how to throw the rug over the withers, folded in half to stop it being unwieldy. He pulled it back to smooth the hair and opened it out. Checking that it lay evenly he then showed them how to thread the back leg straps through each other, so they didn't rub. The rugs were well used, so he buckled up to the wear marks and stood back for the women's admiration.

'That's a lot of work, what if the horses

kick?' asked Mrs Trotter.

'I'm sure they will be fine. I expect these horses were all chosen for being quiet and trustworthy?' He looked at Kathy.

'Yes, they're all lovely Mrs T.'

'Well, we'll now rug them all up, tie them up in the stables and then turn out. I'll come and check then help you.'

All rugged up with no problems. He saw the ladies putting hats on. He chuckled to himself; BHS rubbish again. He walked to the field gate and opened it, pinning it back.

'Right we'll take the first three. Follow behind each other in your own time.'

He took an excited Doris who knew what was coming. Chris gave her rope a surreptitious yank from the other side. The others came out of the stables and at a brisk march, they walked to the field.

'Right release them!' he shouted at the gate. All had quick release catches on the ropes, so a yank opened them. The three horses shot off at a rate of knots, bucking, farting and chasing down to the far end of the field; clods of earth flying into the air as they flew. The other three were immediately jealous and began to bang in unison. Chris could see there might be a problem taking them, so he turned to the others.

'We will have to be more careful. Do you want me to bring them one by one and you do the stables and gates?'

'I think it will be the sensible thing to do so. This doesn't seem so good now. How will we manage on our own?' Mrs T looked more nervous.

'In the future, you will turn them out as soon as they finish work. Only bring them in only when needed.' Boy, he was good at this! All was okay with the next two, although Chris had to dig his heels into the wet ground to try to slow the excited horses down. Both disappeared over the horizon.

Last came the mare he had recognised as one of his own; Breeze. Seeing her name had his heart sinking again because he now remembered her and how bolshy she had been. Why was she here? She had kicked and bitten like a demon when in season and had never been trustworthy. She began kicking seven bells out of the door.

His suspicions were right. Kathy opened the door to let Chris in and Breeze reared up, narrowly missing her head on the lintel. She barged out with Chris hanging on for dear life. Mrs T at the gate reopened it, at the same moment that the other horses came over the hill at full gallop on a return run. Chris could do nothing but let the release go.

The totally wound up horses came slamming through the gate, pinning Mrs T to the wall. They exploded into the yard with a fury of hair, mud, and hooves. Breeze neighed frantically as she reared again and Spot span around to kick her. After a furious melee of snapping and kicking, the herd as one took off and bolted out again: Mrs T now nearly falling over as they tore through the gate. She slammed the gate after them and began to open her mouth to say something that matched the now furious look on her face.

Then she stopped and looked aghast. On the far side of the yard lay Sue. She had been unseen by Chris and had been caught in the melee. They all rushed over to find her unconscious.

'Don't move her!' commanded Kathy. She checked Sue's pulse. 'Ambulance now.' Mrs T dialled frantically. 'Fetch some rugs to keep her warm.' Chris obeyed, and they all stood in silence, not knowing what to say.

'How did she get in the middle of all that?' asked Chris, breaking the impasse. 'Last I saw her; she was heading to the tack room with the ropes.'

'She returned as you came out. You didn't warn us you were coming out, and she jumped back as Breeze reared. I think she kicked out when she came down and you released her. Then as Breeze swung around, she knocked Sue over, and she got trampled. If you had warned us that the horse was exiting, this would never have happened,' yelled Kathy. 'At least she still had her hat on.'

'Yes, if you had shouted, I could have shut the gate.' Mrs T was purple with rage.

'But I would have shouted for you to open the gate!' That shut her up for a moment.

'Sue should have stayed put rather than

getting in the way. She saw they were all getting wound up and should have stayed out the way. She is supposed to be your horse expert.' Chris said at the top of his voice.

At this point, Sue began to groan and shift restlessly.

'What happened? One minute I was coming across the yard to you, the next minute I had a horse in my face knocking me over.' The other two looked at Chris in just retribution.

'I didn't see you as I came out. You came up on my blind side. I thought you were in the tack room. You got knocked over and trampled by the other horses as they all galloped back in again,' stuttered Chris.

'If you'd shouted...' Sue fell unconscious again. To Chris's relief, they could now hear the sound of a vehicle coming down the road. It was the ambulance.

'Looks like we were lucky, they can take longer,' muttered Kathy.
The paramedics swooped in, shoving them away, and loaded Sue onto a body board with a neck brace. They drove swiftly away after Kathy had given an explanation.

Chris stood there feeling hopeless, useless and condemned. As soon as the ambulance drove away, the other two turned on Chris.

'This is all your fault, so you better be here daily until we get someone properly qualified. I don't know how we will cope without her. I expect the horses ready for the first appointment at ten tomorrow.' They strode away without a word, bristling with indignation.

Like a zombie, Chris cleared the stables, closed. All seemed secure. He had no keys, but he wasn't going to chase after Kathy. He collected Rex from the empty stable he had popped him in. He fell to his knees and hugged the shaggy hair as Rex whined and tried to lick to comfort him.

They walked down the hill where the horses were now grazing as if they had never galloped around like loonies in their entire lives. The sea air and beauty circled around Chris as he plodded down this lane; the darkness crawled around his soul. Once back in the cottage he felt more trapped than he had ever been in his life.

At least the farm had been his choice. Now he had to stay; see the cripples and live with his own hideousness, his stupidity. Why hadn't he simply walked away and said no? Left them to manage the horses. Why hadn't he looked? Why hadn't he shouted? He replayed the scene in his mind over and over again. Nothing would change it, but he kept on seeing Sue's pale face and knew he was responsible for the accident. He didn't even have her surname to ring the hospital to get some news.

Alan walked in and found Chris curled up on the sofa. 'What happened?'
And because Alan was Chris's soulmate, he had someone to confide in, a friend who would be

unjudgemental. He told Alan all, sparing nothing; even telling him about the voice. As he talked, Alan put an arm around him.

'You are not responsible for all of that. If this Sue was a proper horse person, she should have known you were coming out of the stable and that the horses were kicking off. Yes, possibly you should have shouted, and you will have to live with that. It's part of the rubbish bit of life.

You were thrust into a situation that wasn't your fault. June has a responsibility in that too. Kathy has a part for expecting you to step in. You must let this run its course and then move on. I'll ring the hospital and find out how Sue is. I can use my vicar status to swing things and we've had, erm, situations with some of our other guests, the staff do know me.'

Chris remained hunched on the sofa while Alan did just that. He only got one side of the conversation, so he hunched more and more in fear.

'She has a broken arm, that's all. No concussion, but a bad headache. No brain damage because of the hat. She's already gone home in plaster to rest. Cheer up mate, it'll be okay.' Alan tried to make eye contact with Chris.

'But I'm stuffed, aren't I? I'm going to have to go every day to do my penance. Those two won't let up. So much for the healing time and moving on. I'm stuck with flaming horses again.'

'Chris, you can go on whining in self-pity

as long as you like, or you can man-up. I hate that expression, but it works. Get on with it, put your plans on hold for a while. You don't have a deadline. Learn from all of this. We're still here, our community is with you. Think about it, supper is in ten minutes.'

Alan left him. Chris sat, the eddies of pity and pain whirling around him. He prayed the most successful prayer ever known to mankind. 'Help, Jesus, help me.'

The next morning had Chris and Rex striding back up that hill again. This time, he was ready, he would see this out. He would take his responsibility and he would stand his ground. He would bring in the horses before they started on him, apologise and get on with his sentence. All this gave him a determination he had never known before. He found the appointments diary in the tack room and read he needed to get in the two horses needed for the morning session. He strode down the field, head collars and some apples.

Spot munched away, facing away from Chris. His ears pricked towards him, his head came up and Spot glared at Chris. He offered the apple, but Spot snorted and turned his back. As Chris came around, Spot finally had enough and took off at a speed towards the end. Chris's spirits sank. He wasn't going to chase the stupid animal around the field. A picture came in his mind of his father and the herd of cobs at home.

He swiftly strode back, put haynets in the stables and got a feed bucket. Then he noisily walked about the yard, shaking it so the nuts rattled about. The wind blew in the right direction. His voice flew with it as he called, 'COOOOOME ON!' over and over again. Chris pinned each door open.

He heard the pounding of hooves and in a matter of minutes, the now muddy herd thundered in. They understood perfectly well which stable belonged to who and that there was food; even though Doris and Spot misjudged. Spot shot out. It took a few seconds to slam the doors shut. Success! He whipped the rugs off the two he needed and did his best to clear the mud. Only Breeze had work in the afternoon, so as soon as the other three had finished eating, he frog-marched them out and slammed the gate.

As Kathy drove in, the horses were clean and still munching on hay. Right now he had to get in first. 'Morning Kathy, I'm so pleased to hear that Sue isn't badly injured. I'm going to visit her this afternoon. Yes, I admit I had a major part to play and I am sorry, but we must move on if we are to work together. Now, the horses are all in, but I don't know what tack you need. You will have to show me.'

She had her mouth open, looking a little

like a goldfish. 'Right, yes, I suppose you're right. I realised last night that I should have warned her. I saw her. We all say things in the heat of the moment. I also realised that we probably don't need you all day either if you leave the lunches for the horses. For at least the next couple of days, we need your strength with turning out until we have a new routine sorted.' Chris agreed and similarly gave Mrs T the full on treatment when she arrived; faced with an apology and being told to do things, she trotted off, if not happily she was under a truce. The morning became organised, and he left the team working if not completely happy.

Chris now had the biggest hurdle of all to jump. Driving slowly into Swanage along the narrow streets of white stoned terraces, he wondered what he was going to say. Finding Sue's house wasn't a problem, but there was no parking outside.

He drove back to the station and used the opportunity to buy needless presents, flowers, chocolates, and magazines. He scrambled with them at Sue's front door. Suddenly it opened. A fierce woman glared at him. 'What?'

'I've come to see Sue; I understand she lives here?'

'She's in no 2 on the top floor. Boots off and no loud noises!' Chris dropped the gifts as he undid his muddy boots and stumbled upstairs; not a good start. He tapped nervously, and the door swung open. Sue sat on a sofa, looking pale, with a huge plaster on her arm.

She turned and smiled. 'Wow, it's not my birthday!' Nevertheless, she reached out a hand for the largess. 'Chocolates, brilliant! I was thinking I fancied something sweet.' Chris handed them over.

'Have a pew!' She unsuccessfully tried to open the box, so he took it and did the honours. He sat down as she gleefully rummaged in the chocolates.

'I've, um, come to apologise for the whole thing. I should have shouted and warned you.'

'Aw, nuts, Kathy should have yelled. You had your hands full with Breeze. She's always a pain in the neck. The person on the latch should be in charge, not the man on the rope, and I should have realised there would be trouble turning them out after such a long time.'

Chris was amazed, he had expected a torrent of abuse at least. He had on more than occasion needed to grovel to Mollie when he had forgotten to tell her that she needed to milk. She hadn't held back at all about what was in her head.

'But you're crocked, what about your job? Will you get sick pay?'

'I'm sort of on the dole, I get this paid for...I'm on a Youth Crime prevention programme. Eustace is my mentor.'

'What did you do?' Help, he said that before

he could stop it.

She grinned. 'Mugging grannies! No seriously, I've had a few problems at home, and I started shoplifting. I've only got a few months more. When I turn 18, I'm off. Eustace has promised me a job, but first I have to behave and then go and get my Riding for the Disabled Coach's certificate. After that, I can run the yard.'

'And you are June's successor?'

'Well, if she hadn't disappeared like that; it was all planned. I usually come over so she gets a day off, I could do that at least. Now she's taken off, I suppose at the minimum you can cover for her.'

'I have no intention of staying. I was trying to escape animals and sort myself out.'

'Kathy said you are the new yard manager!'

'Not likely,' said Chris.

'Where does that leave things?'

'I am working out a better routine. As you know, all the horses will be out, on rubber mats and not fed so much. I'll help with the morning and evening stable, but not more.'

'What about the vaulting?'

'The what?' He'd forgotten.

'That stuff with the surcingle and kids doing that daft stuff we did.'

'And?'

'I'm the only one that can lunge and run the sessions. Kathy does the instructing. Without me, they will need to cancel at least three sessions each week. Can you lunge?'

Chris wanted to lie, but he wouldn't; he owed her something. 'Yes, but not very well, we used to use it to calm the youngsters down before we put a saddle or a rider on them for the first time.'

'Well, if you would get the horses ready, I'll be there to help verbally. It will work.'
She beamed with enthusiasm. Chris swallowed; the doors were closing again. Despite what Sue said; he knew deep down inside he was responsible, so he had to go with it.

'How will you get there?'

'On the bus like I do usually.'

'Are you certain? You still seem very pale and that is a big plaster.'

'Well, you'll have to pick me up then!' That served him right, oh if only he had his truck. Sue ate chocolates like a Labrador. Maybe he would have to buy more. 'Is there anything you want?'

'Sorry, I am pigging out!' She proffered the box. There was a sudden bang on the door and Mrs Grumpy marched in.

'Just checking you're okay? Do you need the painkillers? It's time if you do.' Perhaps she wasn't so bad after all.

'Yes, it is rather sore.'

'Now, young man, I think it's time for you to go.'

'This is Chris, he's another one of the people staying at Eustace's place. He's going to pick me up, and do the lunging while I heal, isn't that great? I'll be able to keep on!' A hint of a smile crossed the woman's face. 'Well, possibly that's all right. I'll have to clear that with Kathy. You mustn't overdo it; that's a bad break.'

'I'll bounce back Mrs Young! Chris, collect next week on Monday about 8.30?'

'Well, I'll come over as soon as I have the horses ready, and I will have to ask the others about using the mini. I wish June hadn't pinched my truck.'

'She did what?' interjected Mrs Young. 'Always trouble that one. Let me ask around.' Completely surprised, Chris swapped phone numbers with Sue and left. Afternoon stables passed quietly and as the sun set, he and Rex walked back to the cottages to more surprises. Sam was waiting for him.

'No more messing about! It's time for you to learn to cook. We're starting with a shepherd's pie.'

To his huge amazement, Chris found cooking surprisingly easy, and apart from the mash having a few lumps; the others praised his work.

Monday morning had Chris honking outside Sue's front door, and she came outside gingerly, with a smile on her face. It was a bit tight getting her and the plaster in, but it worked.

'This is so brilliant. I really didn't want to miss the sessions, I've worked so hard with these groups. Did you get some time off at the weekend?'

'It wasn't as bad as I thought it would be with the horses out, I checked them in the morning, then Alan popped up in the evening. I took the coast path and walked towards Swanage. I found it incredible, walking with the sea on one side and those hills on the other. It makes where I come from seem a little dull and flat.'

'Where?'

'A small village called Hazeley. It's west of Southampton. I have a farm with dairy cows on the estate. We used to breed cobs too, but my parents died in a road accident.'

'Oh, I'm sorry, mine divorced when I was a kid and there's been a long succession of boyfriends since then. I've no idea where Dad is. So why are you at Eustace's?'

Chris swallowed; he'd never told a stranger his story. Maybe it was time, but under his own rules. This kid didn't need to get the full details. He paused.

'Don't worry, everyone at the cottages has a tale to tell. While I'm normally very nosey and want to know, no pressure!' They laughed and drove into the stable yard. Sue had even more trouble getting the plaster and herself out of the mini. Once freed and giggling at the struggle, they saw Mrs T bearing down on them with a tight grin.

'Time's running away. I've cleaned the horse, but you must do the rest!' Not a word of asking how Sue was. She muttered something under her breath, but they made their way to the tack room and collected the gear.

'Why are you using Breeze? She was always unreliable and especially when she's in season,' asked Chris.

'Have you not heard of miserable mare supplement? She has a hormone imbalance, and we don't use her when she's nutty like that. She's not such an old bat!' Sue smiled as she stroked Breeze, who was nibbling the plaster. Chris remembered the tacking up routine and there was only one alteration as he had got the colour order wrong on the legs. They were soon ready. He led Breeze into the school and sent her out on the line. Sue got assertive.

'Now send her out into a good brisk trot, just in case she's got any flies under her tail.' Chris obeyed and with a flick of her heels, she strode out. Once she moved freely, he changed the rein where he found her stiffer but happy to work.

'She certainly is better than when we had her!' He brought her into the middle and Sue came in. 'What you will need to do is get her on a steady walk to start with, and when prompted, raise the lunge whip. One of the kids will judge the right moment to come in and they will stand behind you. When ready, you raise again, they walk down the line to the horse. I'll do the rest of the instructions and yell when I need a change of speed or direction. OK?'

'Sounds fine to me.' A minibus drove in and disgorged the kids. Chris looked at them more closely and at first, didn't think there was anything different about them. Then he saw the Downs syndrome, the slightly irregular features, the slight lack of co-ordination, the offline movement.

But they were all smiling and joking with each other; obviously keen to get on. They saw Sue and began crowding around her, one of the girls even burst into tears. The leader of the group intervened, and Sue told them the story- in which, to Chris's interest, she didn't say which horse. After a while they calmed, and the leader took them into the school.

'Now, this is Chris, he's lunging today, but Sue will instruct you, so you're going to have to listen. No going into dreamland, Lucy!' One girl grinned and hid her face. 'Now seeing as we've had a bit of excitement, all of you, leg it once around the school. After that we will do our stretches... keep to the edge!' They all took off at various speeds and gaits.

'Hi, I'm Jane,' smiled their teacher. 'So glad you could help. They would have hated to miss the session. I'll hang in here this first time as they get to know you. Watch out for Tim; the tall gangly one, he takes a while to accept new people. He might either ignore you or get right in your personal space. Right guys, back to me and stretch.'

While they were doing this, Chris took the opportunity to get Breeze moving again. Sue called, and he raised the whip. He only realised one kid was in when he heard the breathing behind him. He raised the whip again and the first one walked down the line and walked with her hand on the horse's shoulder; matching her footfall to the horse. Soon all six sat on Breeze, two at the head, two shoulders, two hips. They proceeded with a few giggles, casting glances at Chris.

He jumped when Sue's voice came from outside. 'Now prepare for a trot. Keep your heads up. Chris, when you're ready.' He pushed Breeze forward with a click, she understood her job and went into a very slow steady trot. They kept this up for a few circles, then returned to a walk.

'Prepare to leave the circle, starting with Tim.' They knew this job too and one by one, they fell back along their positions to follow the horse. When all six were behind her, they slowed and filed out from the last one. Chris was impressed and said so. 'How long have they been doing it?'

'We do speak, you know,' interrupted an annoyed voice.

'I do beg your pardon, sir!' laughed Chris, hoping this was the right thing to do. 'Tell me! `

'We've been doing this exercise ever since we started this course, which is for twelve weeks; with one week off for half term. Each session lasts about 45 minutes and consists of ground exercises to promote our co-ordination and flexibility. We're now going to do mounted exercises, and I am going first as it's my turn.'

'Thanks, Tim! Demonstrate to Chris

please.' Jane came in, so Chris brought Breeze to a halt and Jane held her head. 'Keep her steady. In a minute, Tim will mount at a walk.' Tim standing at Breeze's shoulders, facing forwards swung his inner leg back and, and with no effort he was up on the horse, holding the handlebars.

'I am going to do Around the world.' With legs stretched, he did the familiar riding school exercise, turning to each side, facing backwards and facing the front. 'Now scissors.' He lay forwards and did such a rapid, contorted flip, Chris didn't quite get it.

Tim continued. 'Now I will stand.' He brought his knees up, knelt and then stood. 'You can walk the horse now,' he ordered. Chris looked askance at Jane, who nodded. Tim wobbled from side to side as she moved off, but he stood tall with his knees bent; rocking to the horse's stride. He didn't look at anyone, but straight ahead, arms stretched out with a fixed expression on his face.

'Oy, Tim, we want a go too!' yelled one, and Tim's face furrowed with annoyance. 'I'm not finished yet.'

'Yes, you are Tim. Prepare to dismount from behind now,' said Jane. He didn't argue, but knelt back down again. He lay and slid down over Breeze's hindquarters to the ground; walking behind her until he could walk out.

'I think that was satisfactory, but I need to work on my mounting.' He wasn't talking to anyone but himself. The session then took all the others going through the same exercises with different amounts of success. Chris saw that Breeze was starting to tense up with the last girl who had Downs syndrome. Her movements were hard and quick.

'It is time to bring today to a close,' Chris suggested. Sue was looking at the mare too. 'I agree. Please, all of you come in and thank Breeze.' They all needed no second bidding and came rushing in and engulfed her in hugs, pats and the odd kiss. She seemed to enjoy it, even rubbing her nose on them and relaxing.

'Please thank Chris who will be here until the holidays,' said Jane. They all came and courteously shook his hand, except for the Down's girl, who he had been told was Maria. She hugged him so hard that he could hardly breathe. Sue had to remind her to let go. Soon they piled into the bus and drove away.

Sue and Chris led Breeze back into her box. 'So, can you cope with them?'

'I think so. What's up with Tim?'

'He has a form of autism which is known as Asperger's syndrome.'

'And Maria?' asked Chris.

'Well, Downs but she also has anger issues. Breeze read that.'

'I've never been close to handicapped people before.'

'Argh, you can't say that anymore. Learning Disabilities will do for now! I've checked

the list. Breeze can go back out after her lunch.'
Chris looked at Sue and saw she was looking pale.
'Are you okay?'

'I'm a bit under the weather and I need some painkillers. They're in my bag in the tack room, would you get them?' Chris hurried to do her bidding.

The two of them got things sorted out, and as they finished, Mrs. T and Kathy came over with another helper. They had been taking a single client around the other end of the school. They were all over Sue, who Chris could see hated it. She didn't like all the clucking and mothering. He saw some glares still being aimed at him, so he butted in.

'I have the idea that Sue needs to go and rest. I'll take her back to Swanage and return to turn out later if that's ok?' He looked at Kathy, who nodded. As they drove back along the coast road, Sue seemed to perk up.

'I hope I'll be able to lunge again before the holidays. Thanks so much. They're a nice lot when you get to know them.'

'I've never had any contact with people like this before. Is this what vaulting is all about?'

'No, this is remedial vaulting in that it is about helping the students, not an acrobatic discipline like it is with the mainstream. The able-bodied kids do all sorts of leaping about; standing on the horse and doing things in canter.'

'I must research it! How did you get into it?'

'When I was in a secure unit for a while, it was about the only thing we were let out for as my supervisor did it in her spare time. It really helped me as it got me moving about; stopped thinking about myself and gave me an interest. And I fell in love with horses. It helped to move me out of there, and when I heard about Eustace, I got him to step in. Still, I'll soon be free of the system and off to train.'

They turned into her street and parked behind an old truck. Something caught Chris's eye as he got out to help Sue out of the cramped car.

'Sue, wow! It's my truck. And it's clean!' He hurried to look around, and even the flatbed was spotless.

'Found in a car pound in Basingstoke. Didn't you think to check?' It was Mrs Grumpy as Chris called her in his head.

'How did you drive it here?'

'Got my layabout son and one of his mates to get it.'

'How much do I owe you?'

'Nothing, except for my son's petrol.'

Something dawned. 'Eustace?' She nodded. It seemed he was going to be in debt to this elusive millionaire – well, he must be with all this philanthropy. He looked around his truck some more. 'I'll take the mini back and come and collect it this afternoon. Is that okay?'

'No problem for me. I guess you might have the keys? My son was totally embarrassed until someone at the yard pointed out the way to start it!' She almost smiled.

'Well, us farmers need things we can leap into. We're always dropping things like keys in the mud!' Chris laughed. 'Any sign of June?'

'None, she has done a good runner this time. She abandoned this on a street where I guess she worked out that it would be quickly towed away. But she had cleaned it, that was always her trademark. Mess up her life but everything in order around it. So it goes on. Right, now, madam, you're looking as white as a sheet. You're going down to casualty with me to get that plaster checked. I said it was too tight in the first place.' The two disappeared into the house arguing. Chris shook his head, looked fondly at the truck, and drove back to turn the horses out.

The following day didn't need him except for basic duties and so he decided to walk the coast path again. The freedom of having his own vehicle, with the legroom compared to the cramped mini made him want to roam. It was most odd.

This new passion for walking had also taken him by surprise. It was not having to rely on four hooves, watch for scary things or how the ground lay underfoot. Freedom to go where he wanted. He talked Alan into coming with too; not that he needed much persuasion. It was one of those special days when the sun shone; the gorse bloomed a late yellow; the grass was greening up.

All seemed well with the world, and that voice was quiet.

They parked near the Square and Compass pub; earmarking it for a pint on their return and made their way down through Worth Matravers. They had admired the wooden Henge by the car park but didn't see the famous dog on the pub roof.

'It's quiet here at the moment, but at the weekends there are so many walkers, and the pub's crowded. It's so cute. Look at the duck pond! You'd think it a film set,' laughed Alan.

'Is it all incomers?'

'A good majority these days. But the farms are still farms, even if they do B&B. Talking about that, have you heard from Mollie?'

'Not a thing, she's a texter, and you made me sling the phone! But I guess if the first lot of girls had been a disaster, I'd have heard. She knows where I am. It'll be the Easter holidays when she has them for two weeks. That will be interesting. I'm glad I won't be there for the onslaught!'

'Are you okay with her using your place?'

'I'm not at all bothered. I'm seeing how my life was confined and narrow. To think I might have spent my whole life there and none the wiser makes my blood run cold. I can't even be sure I will go back.'

'But your generation isn't as trapped as before.'

'Thank heavens. You know this is what I imagined when I came here, walking- not that I've ever done much before...having deep philosophical discussions with you and putting my world to rights. Not getting stuck with those horses!'

'We weren't expecting it either. It's taken your mind off yourself in one area.'

'You're right; I've been me, and the people I've met have only seen me. But I've been a bloke to them.'

'Would you turn up one day in a skirt and scare them?'

Chris burst out laughing at what he saw in his mind's eye of how Mrs T would look. 'No, I don't want to be a woman.' Alan said nothing, and they walked on and Chris processed the thought. Then Alan dropped a real bombshell.

'Now that you seem to be enjoying yourself, I need to pose this question. Do you realise you may have a uterus? It is quite normal for intersex people to have both by definition.' Chris stopped in his tracks. 'I can't think about that. I knew and I'm ignoring that bit.'

'Why not?'

'Because I am me.'

'That makes you truly blessed. You haven't been gender assigned and are free. You are a rare, lucky person. But if you now want to move on and form a relationship with someone; what will you say?'

'I won't tell them anything.'

'Isn't that unfair? What if you had a

relationship, and they wanted to take things further; make a commitment and have a family?' Again, Chris couldn't find an answer and marched on no longer looking at the beauty of the day, his head to the ground.

They strode on in silence down to the quarry. Finally, Alan calling a halt by the caves. They mooched around the quarry buildings and then sat on some half quarried stone. Alan got out a thermos flask. Rex, who had been keeping a low profile; somehow sensing a conflict, now decided it was time to hunt rabbits and took himself off into the undergrowth.

'I fell in love with a man. He loved me too because at that time I was Ann. I played an aloof, hard to get game. I was so afraid of it all coming out; that I would lose him. We would only meet at weekends because of our jobs.

He owns the Star supermarket chain which took him all over the country. I made sure we always met somewhere public and never his place. In that situation, I hoped that the holding of hands and kissing might last forever, and this would be enough. I knew it was wrong, but my fear of him discovering my secret clouded my every judgement. He was a masculine man, and I realised that him finding out would spell the finish of everything. A fool's dream. Have you ever heard the song by the Kinks; Lola? I wanted him to see me as Lola; love person living his life on the other side.

Then one day, he did the thing with the ring box. It was the end for us. He would never deal with my reality. I said no. I ran away, packed my bags and ran off to a friary not far from here. Better that he had a broken heart from a woman not loving him enough to marry him than to see I was a freak. He would be able to have a real relationship.

I sunk myself into God and took orders. I didn't tell them either, which as you understand got me into all sorts of trouble later when I defended you and others. This is why I'm throwing this at you now, while you're safe, where you can fight this and sort yourself out in a secure place; so you don't have to hurt anyone.'

Chris didn't know what to do, suddenly having it all spelt out to him so clearly. He put an arm around Alan's shoulders. He didn't like touching, but had no words either.

'I heard a few years later, Steve had married, but was divorced very soon after. He had no happy end either.' Alan's voice was tinged with real grief.

'But you seem so complete, sorted, being what you want to be from one day to the next.'

'I have found a place where I can be at peace. Helping Eustace's misfits and walking with the Lord. I've even forgiven the doctors; they acted in the good faith of the time. But we know better now.'

'Why aren't you out there campaigning

and fighting for children's rights and helping people like me?'

'I did for a while, but the grief and sorrow ran me dry. I've done my bit. It's for a younger generation to sort out.'

'You're not that old.'

'Look at me, Chris, properly. I'm seventy.' He did.

'But you wear it well! Don't write yourself off!' laughed Chris.

'No, I'm in a place of peace. I will keep that. But I need to help you see things. Maybe I should have left it a while; you've not been here that long.'

'I seem to be finding I like quick answers, so no, it is time. Getting away from the farm has done me a power of good; along with all the new things I've done. I'm set here until Sue's arm is better. That will be at least six weeks. I can enjoy my time. Let me think all this through, it's not going to harm me. I'm stronger now. The demons aren't pursuing me anymore. Let me ponder!'

Alan looked up with a smile. 'You don't know how relieved I am to hear that. I didn't want you jumping off that cliff!'

'And I have the sensation that a weight has lifted through simply telling you it all. That's good.' Chris raised his face to the sunlight.

'Oh no!' Chris groaned and Alan jumped in shock; but it wasn't a sudden revelation. Chris had seen a rapidly approaching Rex, carrying a large, very dead rabbit in his mouth. 'Since when have

Alsatians hunted rabbits?' They both leapt up and had a hard ten minutes chasing the gleeful dog around the undergrowth until he gave the body up in exchange for a sandwich. Alan began telling Chris the history of Purbeck mining and they explored the workings in the Winspit caves.

They made their way to another small bay ringed with sharped ledges. After that, they hiked up the hill back to the village. They enjoyed their pint in a quiet pub and wandered home. Things ran around Chris's head, but not all were to do with his dilemma.

During the next few days, Chris met all the groups who did vaulting and found them so friendly that he greatly enjoyed their sessions. He got over seeing the problems and syndromes. He could now understand them as much more than happy-go-lucky kids. He could almost suck in their happiness.

There were, of course, the odd arguments, typical teenagers, he supposed. The last group was the most advanced, and he had to learn the skill of keeping the horse to a very slow, rhythmical canter for them to leap on and off. One girl even stood for a couple of circuits and got much applause from the group.

'You did good, kid!' laughed Sue. She was much better with a new plaster, off the painkillers and proposing to come on the bus the following week. 'Hey gang, don't you think Chris should have a go?' He caught a wicked twinkle in her eye.

'Peter, can he borrow your pumps? I'll take the line as we'll only walk!' Chris found a pair of smelly plimsoles being proffered to him and knew he was trapped. Peter grinned as they swapped over. Chris walked into the ring, and they all shouted, 'You didn't wait for the whip to go up!'

'She hasn't got one!' he laughed back. Getting on was no problem. Spot's shortness helped and as he had often ridden his ponies bareback; this was fine. He vaulted on and landed behind the surcingle. He remembered too late as the searing pain came into his crotch. He couldn't sit like this, the scars were too painful. Tears ran down his face.

In desperation, he did the round the world movement so he might sit for a moment with his back to the kids and grab a handkerchief. His finally understood how people talked about their eyes watering at such moments. They clapped and cheered, so he swung to the back and returned to the side. How was he going to get out of this? Then it came to him. 'I think I'm going to have a go at standing! Can you come and hold him, Sue?'

She did so and Chris got to his knees with a certain amount of pain but managed to stand without falling. Spot's broad back was wide enough even for his big feet, and he stood right up, his arms outstretched as taught, to a huge cheer.

'Walk, walk, walk, walk!' They were now all calling, so he nodded at Sue. Chris braced himself, so he wobbled with the first steps. Then got the rhythm and relaxed; allowing each hip to dip with the footfall.

It was utterly amazing; he forgot the pain. Talk about high on a horse! He saw the yard from a new perspective. But once around was enough. Sue turned at the right time and stopped. Very gingerly he got down to his knees and slid off sideways, to huge applause. He did a mock bow and come out, only to remember Sue. He went back to get Spot, who knew it was lunchtime.

'That's totally amazed them!' she laughed. 'I guess you need to take off those plimsolls!'

Chris was also impressed now with what the groups did. They seemed to have no fear, no hang-ups and went for it. If only life was that easy. The group hugged and clapped him on the back.

'What was your problem when you sat on the horse, I saw the pain?' asked Sue as they walked back to the yard with Spot. The kids were getting back in their bus. 'I thought you had ridden all your life?' His heart sank. What should he say? He decided on the truth. 'I was assaulted last year, especially in that region and I have a lot of scar tissue there.'

'What happened?' He realised she would not let him fob her off. In his mind's eye, he saw that look on Alan's face. 'I'm not quite what you might think I am. I was born intersex.'

'What's that got to do with anything?'

'I didn't know until recently, and when I found out, I was already right off the rocks. This news sent me off to meet someone in a gay bar. Unfortunately, he arrived late, and I got mixed up with a gay stag/hen do. I got very drunk, and they took me skinny dipping. It seems when they saw me, they saw something wasn't right; they attacked me.' He remembered, as if yesterday, the grin on the man wearing the tiara and the sound of waves crashing on the beach as they laid into him. 'I still have major scarring there, and I'd forgotten about it until today.'

'What's intersex?' Would the questions never stop?

'Please don't make me explain. Google it.' He guessed she'd be running for the bus the next morning when she found out. Shame, he liked her sharpness and enthusiasm about life; despite how things must have been hard for her.

'Oh...you've got the best of both worlds!!' She read on further. 'Have you had lots of horrible operations like it says here, and you don't want to be what you are?'

'No, I was lucky. I owe a huge debt to Alan, our vicar at the time. He stopped them through the courts.'

'You're a bloke?'

'That's who I'm think I am.'

'Cool. I can't see you in a frock.' He had to laugh at that one; if only she knew. Another weight had lifted.

'Are you going to have operations so that you are a real bloke?'

'I haven't faced up to that yet; in many ways I don't want to.'

'What about your scars? You can't go on with those if you want to ride.'

'I'm not sure that I do. I'm thinking about it.'

'I'd be off to the docs yelling for plastic surgery if anything happened to my bits!' she laughed. Chris had the sense that her laugh was a bit hollow. He was laughing with her and cringing inside at the idea of it and her honesty.

'Do you have the internet at your place?' he suddenly asked.

'But of course, why?'

'I didn't bring my laptop and I want to do some research for Alan. Could I use yours for a minute?'

'Come on in. Mrs Grumpy has given you the okay, so she won't throw you out by the neck.'

In Sue's tiny room, she gave him her laptop and filled the kettle. Chris typed in Steve and Star supermarkets.

A few days later, Chris and Sue were on a mission. Tracking down a wealthy man who had run a supermarket chain had been easy. They had then traced him through the old school phone book. It didn't need real detective stuff, but they had found the whole thing quite exciting. He now lived on the outskirts of Basingstoke, and that wasn't a long trip on the motorway.

'Do you think that Alan actually knows where Steve is, after all, he knew about the divorce?' Sue was going around and around the subject.

'Doesn't matter if he does, we need to make that contact.'

'What if he throws us out? I can't get involved with the police again.'

'Well, umm…'

'Spit it out.'

'I rang and made an appointment saying we are students studying marketing and want to talk about the rise and fall of Star,' laughed Chris.

'You cheeky swine! You've bought a phone after all Alan said?'

'I got an old school one without internet on it; only calls and text.'

'Brilliant.' Sue had dragged more and more information out of Chris while they worked together but had given little away of herself.

'So how will you swing the subject to Alan?'

'If you reach behind the seat, I have some notebooks ready. We're going to discuss the success of the supermarket chain and take notes. Then before we get too deep, and he's friends with us; we will ask him about his private life.'

'You know this probably won't work and we'll get slung out when we tell him about Alan/Ann?'

'I owe him.'

They had turned off the motorway and were heading onto the minor roads leading away from the sprawling city. It soon became rich commuter land. Turning down a side lane they came across a tiny cottage that looked as if it needed some care; right out of kilter with the surroundings.

'This doesn't look good.'

'Too late, get the notebooks.'

Chris, with the bit between his teeth, leapt out and pushed the rusty gate. The front door had peeling paint and weeds around the stones. However, the doorbell was new and rang loudly. The door creaked open and there stood a tall elderly man with a beard, wearing a jacket with a red cravat around his neck. Not the old wreck they were expecting.

'Hello, hello! I've been looking forward to your arrival. I've even found you some old advertising you can use!' Deep in guilt, they followed him in. The house was spotless and furnished in new furniture. So much for their original impressions.

'You wondering about the front? It's to keep that nosey, gin and tonic swigging bunch from up the road from thinking I'm one of the gang. They see me as a daft recluse and keep clear when I walk the dogs. I wear old gear too! You okay with dogs?' They nodded and he let two Labradors in who didn't bark but came in, greeted politely, then collapsed by the fireplace. Chris noticed a PC and printer in the corner.

'I'm really sorry about this,' blurted Sue. Chris wished he could kick her. 'We made the appointment under false pretences.'

Steve burst out laughing. 'I worked that out. Didn't you think I wouldn't check you up? Sit down and spill the beans.'

Chris had to step in. 'We came to see you about someone you used to be close to. He's been a mentor to me. I know that he has been deeply unhappy for many years and have the hope that you two would make contact again. You might re-kindle part the friendship. I have the idea that it would make him happy for once in his life. I owe him.'

'Okay, is he an old business colleague?'
Chris looked down, avoiding eye contact. 'I need to explain something. I suffer from a syndrome that has been ignored and hidden for many years. People suffering it have been subjected to what we now see as abuse by the medical world.'

Oh, this was embarrassing, and he saw Steve stiffening up. 'It is what used to be called Hermaphrodite; where one person carries organs of both genders in the body.'

'Yes, I've heard of it. What's it got to do with me?'

Chris started determinedly. 'My, friend, Alan, suffers from this too. It can make you very confused about who you are; especially after incorrect surgery and hormone treatment. He was for a long time more a woman than a man. You knew him as Ann.'

Steve turned white. Silence engulfed the room. A clock ticked merrily in the background and one of the dogs snored.

Steve sort of shook himself out of this shock. 'That explains so much. Thank you for telling me. I think you should go now. I don't know what you hoped to gain from this. Some money to keep this quiet? You're too late on that, and I won't pay.' Chris and Sue stood up as his anger rose.

'We only came to tell you in the hope that you could meet; have a chat and put things to rights. It's played a lot on him and has changed his life. I haven't told him we're here.'

'GET OUT!' Both fled from the roar, bolted into the truck, and took off.

'Well, that went well!' Sue looked pale.

'I thought he might not be pleased,' grinned Chris. 'I've left Alan's phone number and address by the computer!'

Over the next few weeks, as spring came on in relentless bounds, things slowly worked out. The horses shed their winter coats. Multi coloured drifts lay in odd corners of the yard. Chris began to enjoy all the sessions even more; especially the camaraderie of the kids.

They carried their problems lightly; often unaware that they were anything other than normal and with a bunch of mates. Even Tim, intelligent and perfectly aware of his problems, acknowledged them and got on with life. All this worked away like a worm in Chris; told him that he was handicapped, too. Did he look like that on the inside?

He was certain that he now had a good life. There was something that would be done about all of this, but not just yet. He wasn't ready. However, he always found the heavily handicapped clients difficult to cope with. He felt sick inside, and the clouds would try to engulf him again. The only way to keep it away was by prayer.

Chris held onto his new assertion too; especially with Mrs T and it seemed to work well. Although the job had been advertised, there had been few applicants. Those that had come hadn't been suitable. He, Sue, and Kathy had interviewed them, which showed how things had moved on. Sue became a friend as Mollie had never been.

Yet Chris couldn't get to the bottom of how and why it was with them, where they were going. He let it run. Sue was elusive and often troubled at times, but wouldn't open up. She nosily pitched into his life with great interest. In conversations while they worked, she dragged most of his life story out of him; as if living it through him. Sue envied him his parents, the farm and the horses, but not the loss. She even came with him on walks and shared his new love of exploring towns and old bookshops. His cottage was filling with books he read avidly in the quiet evenings. Rex was having a complete ball.

Chris grew into a peaceful pace with Sam and Alan, as they seemed to be morphing into a parental role to him. They had some loud and noisy evenings at the pub and spent time reading and studying the Bible together. In a way, he had a feeling of real peace, but he knew it was a holding place; soon he would have to move on.

Then Eustace returned.

Chris had returned from a walk along the beach with Rex. He bounded about looking for Alan, who had taken to keeping treats for him in his pockets. Someone sat in what they called the sun seat, but from a distance, he couldn't make out who. From the feet of this man, shot out a red cocker spaniel. He had seen Rex and was in no doubt that he was going to sort him out.

The dog came charging along the shore; the man frantically trying to call him back. When the tornado arrived, snapping and snarling; Rex stood there. When he had been a farm dog, there had often been visiting dogs, and he was always passive with them after one large one had attacked him as a pup. The dog tried to bite but got a mouthful of wet hair. He kept on for what seemed like several minutes.

Finally, Rex lost his patience and snapped once with a huge growl, aiming at the spaniel's bum. This caused a terrified yelp and at last the dog backed down. It now grovelled, sinking to ground and whimpering.

'I'm so, so sorry!' The man reached him. 'Jessie is such a stinker, she thinks she owns the place...but wow, look at that!' The two dogs were making friends. Rex even made small jumps of flirtive excitement. They smelled each other, now friends. 'That's never happened before! I'll be blown down! By the way, I'm Eustace!'

Chris looked and saw a middle-aged man with receding hair, sunglasses, and a tan on his face. He was slightly plump, dressed in tweeds and boots, just another wealthy landowner. Chris had built this mysterious figure into something special; but he was ordinary. Eustace proffered his hand, and they shook carefully. Both dogs took off together to check the beach out.

'I've heard a lot about you, and I thank you for letting me stay here.' Chris finally said.

'Oh, it's nothing, I like to help people. I've got too much money and so have fingers in many pies as you have probably guessed,' he laughed at himself. 'I've been in India doing some stuff, but I'm back now for a while to catch up on things. I've found someone to work on the yard until Sue is better. They'll stay and supervise her until she has done her training; so that's all sorted. What do you think of my splendid chargers? I hear from Alan you're much happier now?'

Chris was more than annoyed; but guessed from what Alan and Sam had let slip, Eustace knew and found out all with his concerns. That reminded him.

'And all that happened with June, that she took off like that?'

'I knew you would help, so I told her she could leave. She'd been here long enough and needed to move on. Being her, she did it in her own way stealing your truck! She's up in London working on a project for me.'

Chris was even more annoyed. 'Are you some sort of Machiavellian figure organising all our lives just because you're rich?' Eustace laughed and clapped Chris on the shoulder, almost knocking him over. 'I've never been called that before.' Again, the gut laughter. 'Come and have lunch and we can get to know each other!'
Bemused, Chris did.

Over the meal he found that actually Eustace had a big heart and simply loved to help people. He regaled them with his tales of the new project in India and other things he was working on. The afternoon turned into evening and the empty wine bottles piled up. The dogs returned, tired out; falling asleep together in Rex's basket, a mixture of brown and red hair.

Eustace laughed, 'I think you might have to

leave Rex here with me, these two are in love!'

'At least someone has a happy end,' sneered Alan. That shocked Chris, he'd never seen that side to him, maybe it was the wine. He was also quite befuddled and didn't understand, so Eustace spelt it out. 'Chris mate, it's time for you to go home.'

A few days later, Sam and Alan were again on the cottage seat, enjoying the morning. Rex and Jessie lay sunbathing too, now inseparable. Eustace had left Jessie behind with some regret, but Alan was chuffed to have the dogs. Rex hadn't even missed Chris leaving. Alan looked up the hill to the quarry, shielding his eyes from the sun as he had caught some movement.

'Seems like we've got visitors! Good grief, one of them looks like a nun...' he gulped. 'Oh, my soul, the other one is Steve.' He rose unsteadily to his feet.

MOLLIE

Mollie sat with her head in her hands on the sofa, Her mop of frizzy brown hair fell protectively around her face. Why had she ever thought she could do this? Why had she never considered what it might be like from the other side? She had thought she knew teenagers, what it would be like with them, but today had been a nightmare. Rattie, the black collie cross and Mutantmutt, the multi-coloured mixture sat by her side; sensing her misery. She stroked them absentmindedly as she ran through the day's events in her mind to try to understand where she had gone wrong. It brought no relief.

Sister Jo had been adamant that she would not stay and help the girls settle in and took off with a cloud of dust in the minibus. Perhaps Mollie should have read the warning signs then.

The four girls stood there looking dumbfounded and embarrassed, hugging stuffed backpacks. The youngest had thawed out first; Sarah as Mollie remembered from the notes she had been sent. Twelve. Just on the cusp of it all. The other three were fifth formers and she could see from their body posture that they didn't want to be here, or maybe anywhere at all.

'Right, I'm Mollie, as you know, so come on in and fight over the bedrooms!' She led the way hoping they would follow, and like quiet little sheep they did. She almost felt the hostility as they thumped up the stairs. 'Now, you have a room each, have a look and decide.' They shuffled and looked in each door; Sarah always being the last and getting pushed to the back. Should Mollie make an issue and make the others let her look in the rooms first?

'I'll have this one,' stated the blonde girl. To Mollie's surprise, Sarah butted in, 'I want one that looks over the stables.'

'That's the end door on the left. What about you other two?' They silently grabbed one of the handles each and went to go in. 'Now hold on a minute! The password is written on the board on the back of your doors. All of you have en-suite showers. I'm sorry to say that the water comes from the hill and the pressure isn't high, but it heats on demand so you can have long showers. The water here is hard; you will need more washing stuff than normal. There are extra blankets and pillows in the cupboards. If you need to put up pictures; please not on the exterior walls. They're hard and nothing sticks. Settle in and food is in half an hour.'

The silence was deafening; not golden. Mollie slunk her way downstairs, her heart in her boots. In the kitchen she put the bacon on to fry;

double checking her list that there were no dietary problems. Then she laid the table with the cloth and new plates she hoped they would like. To her relief that none wanted to go to Mass either.

She heard the footsteps on the floors above and wondered what they were all thinking. It took her back to the first time she had been dumped. Although only ten, she had been so awkward; didn't know what to do or say; what she could touch or do, and no one gave her any clues. It was just expected that she understand when mealtimes were and where to leave her boots. OMG, had they brought wellies? She looked out of the window and to her joy saw a line of them abandoned on the yard.

'Um, where do I leave my riding kit?' Debbie stood at the door. The blonde and most scary one.

'Go through that door. There're hooks and stuff.' Mollie had forgotten the dogs, and the utility room opened to a cacophony of noise from Mutantmutt and Ratty. Oh no, she would get mobbed. She waited for the shriek. It didn't come.

'Oh, babies, you're so cute!' she squealed. Debbie sank to the floor to get washed and wagged at with huge enthusiasm. 'What are their names?' Mollie spent a happy couple of minutes telling Debbie all about the dogs then they all came back into the kitchen. Here, the dogs found three more members for their fan club. Eventually, the fun wore off, and the girls looked at Mollie for what's next. This turned out to be burning bacon and clouds of smoke.

'What do I do, chuck it and start again?' said Mollie, trying to sound amused.

'Chuck it, we're vegan!' grimaced Jenny, with the red hair tied back from her face.

'You're what?'

'Yeah, we're doing it for Lent. Didn't Sister Jo tell you?'

'No, she didn't.' Mollie flopped onto her chair. 'What the dickens does vegan mean when I go shopping? All I can give you for lunch now is some vegetable soup.'

'So long as there's no milk in it,' smiled Clare, the last one to speak. She had that look of mischief about her. Mollie had that sinking feeling.

'Are you all having me on?' She now glared at them, but the stares she got back were unwavering.

'Oh, darn it, we'll go to Macdonalds, I suppose they do vegan now?'

'Oh, yes!' they chorused, even Sarah joining in.

'Right then, Jenny.' She had to take control somehow. 'Please, would you put the dogs back in the utility room? They'll go in if you chuck them some of the bacon. Rest of you, we have to go across the yard; you better get those wellies that are standing outside.' Mollie grabbed the Land Rover keys from the wall and strode out. The girls all piled in the back, no one wanting to chat to Mollie. Right, you lot, she thought, take this.

She knew it was being unprofessional, but rats to them.

She took the old road down to the village road, which was unmade and full of potholes, rather than the front one. They bounced and lurched their way down past Hazeley Manor and the stables. She waved at Joanna in the distance who was pushing Amber along in her buggy. She slowed down slightly by the stable yard. Shouting over the engine, 'This is where you will be riding! When we come back, we'll stop off and I'll introduce you to Ann and we can sort out what you want to do.' Mollie hoped she had heard someone say cool, but she couldn't be sure.

Macdonalds was crowded, but the girls disappeared like homing missiles. They rushed straight to the screens; ordered and within minutes were collecting their food. They left Mollie struggling with the new menus. In the end, one of the staff came and sorted her out. By the time she was clutching her tray, all the gang was sat at one table, leaving no room for her. Inwardly fuming, Mollie made her way to a corner and bit into her burger and bacon roll. This was a nightmare; now she had to shop over again for the next ten days. She found a crumpled piece of paper in her pocket and started to write.

'Do you need some help with that? I guess it's a new shopping list?' Debbie whisked it away from her and took it back to their table. This was getting worse and worse. Mollie ate her chips as if they were cardboard. It was just like when she worked at the stables where Tina and the others had run over her all the time; where there was never enough water for her coffee at tea break.

'Right, we've worked out a menu for the week. Where do we shop?' All four were bearing down on her. Mollie swigged the last of her coffee. 'Follow me.'

The supermarket was across the road on the small industrial estate, and they all marched over. Mollie still hadn't seen the list and as they began throwing things into the trolleys, she lost her temper.

'Now stop. RIGHT NOW! I haven't seen your list and I've already stocked up. It's daft to duplicate things.' She snatched the list from Clare's hand. 'Right, we don't need this and this.' She crossed out several things, 'Now what the dickens is this?'

'A vegetable,' drawled Sarah, and Mollie looked up in surprise. She had her down as the sweet one.

'Fine. So how come if you all have school meals, how do you all know so much about cooking vegan?'

'Well, we might be in school, but we are up to date what's going on in the world.' Sarah's tone was now condescending.

Mollie chose to ignore her. 'Right, if you've got everything, we'll go to the checkout.' At the bottom of the trolley were some magazines and beauty products. Mollie removed them and handed them to the girls. 'Not my responsibility!' Unwilling hands took them. Mollie had her cloth bags with her, so at least there weren't any snipes on plastic ones. They all trundled out to the Land Rover and set off.

'Like I said, we're just going to pop into the stables, so you can see the setup and make any bookings you want. The bills will go to your parents, so I guess you should make the best of it!' That fell flat, and it was with relief that she pulled into the yard.

As usual, she had mixed emotions about the place. Yet the Victorian style stables with the green shutters and the horses' heads looking over the doors was like a picture book. It always won her over. Silver looked over the door and even gave her a whicker; someone loved her!

Ann came out of the tack room with a big grin on her face. 'Hi, Mollie, completely at the right time! All the horses are in, so girls, have a look and see what you think. Afterwards, we can get together and plan your rides and lessons.' The girls slouched off.

'What a glum-looking bunch!' she exclaimed. 'I understood they had all chosen to come because of the riding?'

'You wouldn't imagine so, by the looks on their faces! They're a right bunch of miseries; only been here a few hours and they're demanding vegan food.'

Ann grimaced. 'Rather you than me!'

The girls made their way down the stables finally showing some signs of animation. Sarah was talking to a bay pony who had his nose in her pockets. Maybe there was some hope. The other three were looking at a large thoroughbred who chose to ignore them.

'Right ladies, tell me all the details of your riding life so I can match you to the best horse,' Ann interrupted.

'Well, I only ride thoroughbreds, so I guess this one's for me,' said Debbie in a condescending tone. 'I've done all my Pony club tests and I want to ride professionally as a dressage rider.'

'Ok, so only school work for you, not interested in hacking out.'

'No, not my thing…'

'I like to hack out, but my love is jumping.' Jenny showed signs of animation at last. 'Me too,' chorused Clare.

'What about you?'

'Well, I guess a little of everything.' Sarah was still standing by the pony.

'Right, well, with so many talents, I suggest we should all start with a lesson tomorrow morning. Then you can get to know the horses and see which ones you like. I will allocate for this session; afterwards we'll discuss it. Please, could you be here by 10 to tack up?'

Mollie watched Debbie open her mouth as if to protest but resisting it. The others nodded.

Ann tipped Mollie a wicked wink, and for the first time, her spirits lifted; someone was on her side.

Back at the farm, Mollie stopped them heading for the house. 'I need to show you around so you know what's going on. Follow me. This place used to be run as a stud for cobs, so there are four stables at the back here with a tack room and a foaling box. Beside this is the barn and milking parlour.' She waved her hands in that direction and saw the girls curling their lips and making gagging faces.

'It's a farm, you'll get used to it. I milk once a day, depending on whether we need some milk or if someone's looking full of milk. There are four calves and cows here at the moment. If any of you would like to watch the milking or take part, just say. It's great fun and I can teach you how to hand milk too. Here is the barn where they come into if it looks like rain. The joke fell flat; they obviously weren't country girls. 'Up the hill behind is a path to an amazing viewpoint, and you can walk the dogs or mooch. Most of the fields here belong to us and Hazeley Manor, which is the other side of here, so please feel free.' No interest. 'Now these are the main paddocks. Here is Keith, the stallion and his two mares, who will soon foal.'

Mollie whistled through her fingers causing the girls to cringe. From the field came an imperious neigh, and Keith came down, followed by his harem. Although his winter coat was coming out, his scars made his palomino coat appear threadbare and scruffy.

Before they could sneer, Mollie began with a warning note in her voice. 'He was badly injured last year in an accident when he bolted and jumped two wire fences. The rope caught, and he fell. We nearly lost him. Don't write him off for being slightly lame either. He comes from a very rare bloodline and his foals are worth a pretty penny.'

At this, they went to the fence and began stroking him. Shallow lot, thought Mollie. But Keith, ever one to be admired, enjoyed all the attention. 'The mares should foal around Easter. It will be interesting to see what colour they come out as both of these carry piebald genes. Now, let's unload the Land Rover.'

All the shopping was dumped on the kitchen table; the girls being more interested in greeting the long-imprisoned dogs. They then all sidled off, leaving Mollie to unpack. That done, she took the dogs for a run around and let Queenie out who she had kept in for a milking demonstration.

Soon it was time to make an evening meal; the bacon bun had been a long time ago. Mollie in preparation for the unfilling meal swiftly ate a large chunk of the cake she had made for the girls. She realised she didn't have a clue about what to prepare, so she stood at the foot of the stairs and banged the dinner gong she had prepared earlier. That got them out of their rooms, and the surprised looks on their faces when they came into the kitchen made up for the rest of the rubbish day. It seemed they had expected the meal to appear as if by magic.

'Now, I don't know anything about cooking this stuff. I've never eaten vegan. You will have to show me.' All four had horrified expressions.

'But we don't cook it at school; it's an option.'

'Did you expect me to magic it up? Right, you've all got phones, go online and find out how we're going to cook this stuff and what we need.'

That had them scurrying for their screens, and then a heated discussion followed between themselves about what they wanted.

'Go ahead, all the cooking equipment is at your disposal.' Mollie sat in the old armchair and let them bicker and argue the meal into life. It was interesting to watch the dynamics; Debbie was bossy and autocratic; Clare kept on cracking jokes and dropping things, while Jenny just followed orders. Surprisingly, Sarah from behind, organised and manipulated them into doing the recipe she had chosen. Most interesting. But it was like Mollie had vanished. They only included her when they couldn't find the plates.

A concoction of nuts, vegetables and sauce was dumped on each plate and they set to. It's not a bad thought Mollie, and it was actually quite filling. The girls ate with minimum discussion, threw everything into the dishwasher and disappeared. Mollie cleared what they had missed and sat in a heap on the sofa. Why were they like this when they had chosen to come? What could she do better? How might she break the ice? Had she been the same? Her memories were dim. Her phone rang, it was Gary. What a relief to hear his deep rumbling voice and talk to a salient human being. In her minds' eye she saw his huge, comforting bulk, kind eyes and gentle grin.

'Have they settled in okay?'

'They're a bunch of uncommunicative, manipulative bitches. I don't know why they even asked to come here! They've demanded to eat vegan, so I made them cook it after we had to do another shopping trip.'

'Speak up a bit. I'm sure they can't hear you! Bill the parents!'

'They blank me the whole time and are spending the evening locked in their bedrooms.'

'Takes livestock a while to settle in, give them time!' chuckled Gary.

'They're riding tomorrow. That may cheer them up, but only until they find out I'll be with them! One of Ann's girls is on a course, so I'm helping out!'

He laughed. 'Are we still on for lunch at the pub on Sunday?'

'Too right, they're on a day's ride! I need my roasts after being force fed nuts! Did you get the fields sown okay and did the sheep sell for a good price?' Then followed a normal farming, flirting conversation, and Mollie fell asleep that night with a happier heart.

Early the next morning, before she heard any stirrings from the girls, Mollie walked the dogs along the lane. She needed some fresh air and quietness to organise her thoughts and try to prepare herself for the onslaught. As Mutant and Ratty leapt around hunting rabbits, she decided on being cheerful, not to try to draw them out.

Like the cows; give them time to settle in and then possibly the horses would make them happier still. When she got into the kitchen, to her surprise, they were all seated at the table; munching healthy breakfasts and chatting together. Of course, they greeted the dogs first, which put them up in her estimation. They all chorused a 'Good morning.' Mollie was gobsmacked.

'You all seem more cheerful today!' She grinned despite putting her foot in her mouth with the comment.

'We were all so tired yesterday; we'd all been up late the night before with the last night dance,' smiled Clare. 'What time do we go down to the stables?'

'Crumbs, it's later than I thought; in about half an hour.' She quickly poured a cuppa, but the tea looked a murky green. 'What on earth is this?'

'Green tea, much better than that ordinary stuff.' Mollie took a sip. It tasted disgusting. 'No, not for me!' The girls just looked, so she made a cup of proper tea and sat down. 'What would you like to do this afternoon?' Again, they all looked at each other, Mollie smelt conspiracy.

'Um, could we go into Southampton to do some shopping?'

'Don't you get enough of the place during term time?'

'Yeah, but the old crows are always restricting where and what we do.'

'Should I be concerned?'

'Aw, come on, we want to go for as long as we can and take our time; it's always, hurry up girls, blah, blah blah,' moaned Jenny.

That Mollie did remember. And the parents had put permission to roam on the forms. 'Ok, I'll take you to the bus stop for the 1.30 and then pick you up depending which one you get back again.'

'What, can't you take us?'

'I'm not a taxi service, and the Land Rover is slower than the bus. You all have enough money, don't you?' Another shared glance, and they nodded. 'Right, I'll load the dishwasher and you can get your gear sorted.' They didn't argue that one and were soon ready to go.

Ann waited in the yard, looking very serious with a clipboard under her arm. 'Right, you all need to sign these stupid forms that the school sent. After that we can tack up…Debbie isn't it?

Please take those spurs off, no one wears them here.'

'But I'm a dressage rider and we must have these for clear aids.'

'Oh no, you don't. Any real rider can do dressage without tack at all. You take them off or you can't ride!'

With a massive sulk on her face, Debbie obeyed and slung them in the back of the Land Rover.

'Right, you're lucky today we got your horses in, but normally, you will be expected to fetch them. They're clean too, so we need to go and get tack. All the headcollars are hung outside the doors.'

They all trooped in and got their tack, Mollie and Ann exchanged grins as Mollie realised which horses had been allocated. The girls laden with leather were directed to stables. They all passed the first test, putting the tack neatly on the door and going in with headcollars. Mollie couldn't resist loitering near Debbie, and as she had expected there shortly came an explosion.

'I'm not riding this!' She swung out of the stable. 'I've never ridden a cob in my life, especially one that is so fat and hairy! I want a thoroughbred!'

'It's Maisie to you, and for your information, she won the Pony club dressage championship last summer!' Ann was on her case. 'It's her or nothing. I need to assess how you all ride.' Debbie stalked back to the tack room.

Mollie heard sniggering from the next box

and looked in. Sarah, although the youngest was as tall as the rest. She was tacking up an elegant bay mare of around fifteen hands. She grinned at Mollie. 'Serves her right. She always gets the best horse.' They exchanged a grin. Sarah seemed well able, so Mollie checked the others.

Clare was nearly ready, but her horse swung around the box as she tried to do the girth up. Again, Ann had got it right, the aptly named Fidget was up to her usual. Mollie opened the door. 'She tries all her tricks out on you, so just watch her. She's half Arab and very intelligent! Clare laughed, 'I got the idea!' Mollie held her while Clare did the girth and left her to it.

Lastly, Jenny was measuring her stirrups on a broad bay mare who was dozing. Even so, her hands shook a bit, but Rosy didn't pick it up. How had Ann got them so swiftly assessed?

'If you're not going to ride Debbie, please, will you untie Maisie and give her a haynet? They're around the back.' Ann now joined them, ready for business with her hat on. 'Right, now please remember to push the doors hard open as you come out; they will catch and not swing back on you. Lead from the shoulders and go down to the arena.'

Mollie and Ann led in and as the girls lined up, they checked stirrups and girths. Once they were mounted, Mollie didn't want to be in the way, so she sat in the judge's box and watched. She hadn't seen Ann teach before, and it certainly was interesting. She had the horses all warmed up and keeping good distances then changed the rein. She was getting them ready for a trot when Debbie came down, pulling a reluctant looking Maisie.

'I'm so glad you came!' Ann appeared genuinely pleased and soon had them in the school. They let Debbie and Maisie go through the gaits and the group had a gentle canter. Mollie stifled a rising giggle as she could see Debbie's legs like windmills, trying to get Maisie to be more active.

Ann pulled them all into the centre and had them put the stirrups up. Torture time! They weren't too bad though in the trot, keeping themselves leaning slightly backwards, helping them to hold their seats and holding their legs in a good position. They had all been well taught. Mollie shared their relief when it ended.

Next was most odd. Ann had them stand in the stirrups in halt and spread their arms. They struggled and couldn't hold it; what a brilliant balance exercise! It got worse as she had them knot the reins and do it in walk, having to push their heels down and legs behind their centre of gravity to keep the balance. It started them giggling as they wobbled and lurched. After a couple of rounds, Ann called them in. Mollie found it difficult to hear, but they smiled and even laughed together. Mollie had a surprising pang of jealousy.

The girls then cantered around on their own and in that, the relationship between horse and rider came out. Debbie nagged at Maisie the whole time, and Ann pulled her back in to show her something with the position of her legs; her stirrups were taken up a hole and this time she got more of a response. Debbie looked almost happy.

Sarah rode a gentle canter around the school, looking blissed out. Fidget was next and napped. She stopped and wouldn't budge. Clare didn't fall for it and sat there. After a few minutes, Fidget huffed and walked on; clever Clare had seen through her tricks. Forewarned is forearmed. She then cantered happily around.

Jenny looked quite pale but managed a slow canter, Rosie going slowly and looking after her. It was now cool down time; Mollie heard the 10.30 ride entering the yard and left to help out.

On the way back, the animation in the Land Rover was pure joy to Mollie. Even Debbie begrudgingly admitted that she had done okay once her leg position improved; but couldn't resist some comments on thoroughbreds. Sarah and Jenny were just loving their horses and Clare laughed at Fidget's tricks. They all piled into the kitchen and made a feast for lunch. Mollie was surprisingly part of the team as they talked about the horses together, and it helped that Mollie knew them; all their habits and quirks.

Then they took off like whirlwinds and returned looking like different girls as they put on clean clothes and makeup. Still, Mollie heaved a sigh of relief as they got on the bus. It was so much more hard work than she had thought. She spent the afternoon pottering around and at last, couldn't resist taking a peak in the girls' rooms.

Pretty much as expected; half unpacked bags, cables and devices, clothes on the floor; magazines and packets of sweets all over the place. This she identified with. The last room was unlike the others. It had order; the bed made, a few clothes hung on the hangars, and not many toiletries in the shower room. A Bible on stood the shelf with books from the Pope and other people. A picture of Jesus leaned on the mirror. It was the room overlooking the yard, so it was Sarah's. Puzzled, Mollie trotted downstairs; it didn't seem right for such a young girl. She glanced at her watch and realised it was time to go to the village.

The bus arrived and rolled away; no girls. Mollie panicked, her heartbeat starting to rise. She checked her phone and there were no messages. She jumped out of her skin as it rang in her hand and Debbie's number came up.

'It's Sarah. She should have met us by the Bargate, and she hasn't turned up. Her phone's off too. What do we do?' For once, she didn't sound that confident.

'Did she say what she was up to?'

'No, we split into groups, but she wanted to go on her own. This is worse than at school,' Debbie wailed. Mollie could hear a conversation in the background.

'It's okay, she's here now.' The phone was

put down and Mollie frantically re-dialled.

'What happened?'

'Can you believe it? She visited a tattoo parlour! Listen, the next bus is coming, we'll be back soon…'

Mollie sat transfixed. What could she do? Should she ring Sister Jo? What might the parents say? This could be the end of all of her project. She faced disaster in the face, but a tiny bit of her was relieved; it hadn't been at all what she had expected.

What to do now? She had an hour to wait. It didn't seem worth returning to the farm, so she drove up to the Manor. She hadn't seen Amber, her Godchild, for a week and missed the cheeky bundle. But no one was in, so she returned to the bus stop and sat and thought about how she should handle all of this; angry, smooth it over, ignore it?

Each time, she tried to predict the outcome and how she would have reacted if it had happened to her as a teenager. None of her scenarios worked, so she ate a bar of chocolate and waited.

The girls bundled off the bus, all laughing at something, and piled in.

Mollie turned, with what she hoped appeared a stern face. 'So, what happened?' They all answered, saying the same thing at once and laughing. Mollie got the gist. Sarah now had a tattoo of the Sacred Bleeding heart on her arm; was adamant her parents wouldn't mind, and it was

ANNA RASHBROOK

her responsibility.

The others found it hugely funny and began discussing what tattoos they might have. It got steadily more outrageous. Debbie was going to have a horse on her back; Clare a David Bowie. In the end, Mollie joined in and said she would have her dogs' names on her bum, which had the biggest laugh of all. While they were all in one place, she had to have her say.

'Now girls, you all dealt with this like adults, but what if one of you had been injured or abducted? I have to be responsible and I'm not going to have my life made a misery because you can't act sensibly.'

'Oh, give over, Mollie, you sound like Sister Jo', moaned Clare.

'But you are here with me. All I ask is a bit of common sense; I don't need to know what you are up to. This is your holiday home. I'm just saying don't do anything that will put us all in grief.' That they got. They lurched out of the Land Rover with bags of shopping and actually showed Mollie some of what they had bought. Mollie loved the colours and styles but had to say she was happier in jeans and t-shirt. After another joint effort at supper, the girls once again vanished into the paintwork. Mollie took a deep breath and went to Sarah's room.

'Coming to give me the once over?' Sarah sat on her bed reading; a belligerent expression on her face.

'Nope. I want to check you used an accredited place.'

'Oh, yes, I checked them out online. It was a good set up.' She relaxed a little.

'And your parents?'

'They won't notice or care.' Mollie warmed to her; she had been in the same place.

'What are you reading?'

'An American evangelist; he's most interesting, but I don't think the Pope would approve. Father Hardy says we should read and judge things against the Holy word.'

'Don't you want to do the makeup thing the others are doing?'

'Not for me, I like the quiet life and they're not in my year.'

'Have you got someone who could come with you another time?'

'Perhaps.'

'What about Mass tomorrow? No one signed up to go. You're out all day.'

'Oh, I did loads of extras so I'm in credit.'

Mollie laughed. 'Building up extra points with God. Do you think he cares how often you parrot the same things at him?'

'No, not really...' She looked uncomfortable at that.

‚Well, tomorrow, we must check your bandage so that it doesn't rub when you're riding.' Mollie didn't know what else to say, so she left. Shutting the door, she glanced back; Sarah was deep in her book, with the oddest expression on her face.

The following morning, even Debbie looked forward to the day's ride to the sea, and Mollie left them all at the yard with a sense of relief. She walked down to the pub and sat in the garden with the dogs waiting for Gary. Maybe it was an overreaction to a new experience and things might be all right.

The dogs were quiet too, so of course, Gary had to sneak up behind her with a loud BOO! that she nearly fell off the bench.

'You, ratbag! I nearly fell flat on my face!' He engulfed her in a warm embrace, and she began to feel better.

'You seem tired out, what's gone wrong now?' he asked

'Nothing except the youngest one took herself off for a tattoo yesterday, and they all missed the bus. They'll be back later this afternoon. They'll all have sore bums then, payback time!' They laughed and made their way indoors. Over a pint, Mollie told him more on how she was feeling out of control and side lined; how it wasn't as she remembered it and it all seemed to be going pear-shaped.

'Listen, this is the first lot. It was always going to be difficult; you probably had this idea of them all being yes and no and a you're so lovely Mollie thing happening.' She hated him for seeing right through her!

'What they need is something that you can all do together; not a chore, something that's fun. I'm sure that will make all the difference.'

'How very profound of you!'

'Na, don't forget my mum ran the Brownies for years. She was always full of team spirit and all that rubbish!'

'How are they, by the way?'

'Moaning that it's too hot already in Spain, some people are never satisfied! Do you want to order?' It was so nice to sit and chat after the loneliness of the past couple of days. That was it. She had felt lonely despite the full house. After a roast, more beer, and a game of darts, Mollie now could take on the girls and make them love her. Gary laughed at her mercurial ideas but got the lonely bit. They walked the dogs by the river, then duty called. The day had seemed such a light relief. For the first time she felt sad to see Gary pile into his car and go, but they would meet at the next weekend. Spring ploughing was in full swing, so he had his hands full too.

The yard was full of ponies and mums, with the Sunday lessons coming to an end as the girls returned. However, they all had smiles on their faces and wanted to tell Mollie about their adventures all at once; Mollie's sore heart was consoled.

She helped them with untacking and putting the horses out. She loved hearing about the galloping and jumping the breakwaters; how Rosy had tried to take Jenny for a swim; the great pub lunch; and yes, how sore their bums were! Ann caught Mollie's eye and they sneaked around the back.

'They are gelling as a group. That Sarah is on some sort of agenda, but when she tries to order them around, they ignore her or tell her to shut up. Debbie is all mouth and trousers; dressage my foot. She's only done one local competition! Clare and Fidget are matched as neither of them can keep still but it works. '

'I wish they would let me in a bit, they all hold me at arm's length. Gary said something about we should find them an activity I can do with them and we can bind as a group.' Mollie knew she was moaning but couldn't help it.

'That's not a bad idea, especially as later this week you will be teaching them; although that isn't the role you want to keep.' Ann looked thoughtful for a moment. 'I've got just the thing. Can you find out if they have some soft soled trainers, like plimsolls we used to wear at school?'

'There's so much junk in the house, I expect they do!'

'Well, bring them down tomorrow morning. No riding gear, but hats and tracksuits, you too…Barney wasn't used much today, so he can have his day off on Tuesday,' she said mysteriously then turned to Mollie with a big grin. 'I think you'll like it, but I will say nothing more!' Mollie had to be content with that as she rounded up the girls and they returned to the farm. Once again, they all disappeared, but this time Mollie took pity on them and made supper. She'd found some fake meat in the fridge, so she made a simple but huge cottage -or was it a bungalow pie?

Whatever it was, the pie disappeared at a rate of knots, along with the vegan ice cream and biscuits. The girls were mystified about what Ann's plan was but did have some suitable footwear. They hadn't discovered the smart TV before, so Mollie spent a wonderful evening being briefed on the channels she was missing; finding herself being signed up for them and laughing at some daft American sitcom. Her heart swelled.

When they arrived the next morning, Ann was lunging a small, round bay cob. He had a surcingle and a large blanket on; this didn't provide many more answers. Ann slowed him and came over to them.

'Have any of you done gymnastics at school?' Their eyes seemed to glaze over at the mere mention of the place, but they nodded. 'Well, this is on horses. You might have seen in the circuses some frilly woman on a horse with a plume on its head cantering and jumping through hoops.

This is what you are going to do, but maybe not the hoops. Vaulting is a major sport in Europe; I saw some competitions when I was in Austria. Check it out on YouTube later. We will start with the basics of getting on and off. Barney is new to this too, so please treat him with respect! Who wants to go first?'

Sarah strode forward. Ann gave her a leg up.

'Right. Now for this time, I will give you a standard leg up, but later, you all will have to swing up from the ground...Sarah, I want you to do the round the world movement from when you first learnt to ride, but now, there's no bending the legs. You must swing from the hips and keep your toes pointed.'

She followed the familiar routine but found it difficult with the handles on the surcingle and roller. Barney stood like a rock as if he knew all about this, but what did surprise him, was when she then did it in the walk. But it wasn't a problem. She then dismounted by swinging her leg over him and coming down to face the front. Most odd.

The other girls did the same to a certain amount of giggling, which got louder when Clare got her leg stuck. Ann changed the rein and upped the odds.

'Right, I take it that was okay? Debbie first this time.'

Once she had mounted, Ann told Debbie she had

to stand on the horse; this caused huge laughter. But slowly and gently, she got up and knelt, then carefully stood. Barney put his ears back but decided again that it wasn't a problem.

'Wow, I can see for miles! His back is very wobbly and soft.' She spread her arms and bent her knees as prompted. 'That's better.'

'Right, now you're going to be Barney's first real customer!'

'What?'

'Barney I'm going to ask him to do a very slow walk. If you sense you're losing it, you must either will sink slowly to your knees not hurting him or carefully jump off onto the ground. You up for it?' She nodded.

Ann sent Barney forward but after the first two steps, he stopped in puzzlement. 'Mollie, can you lead him?' Gently she took his noseband, and this gave him confidence. Debbie whimpered a little but stayed put on top. After one circuit, Ann stopped him. 'Right now, off with a jump or knees?'

To a huge cheer, Debbie leapt off Barney and landed on the ground on bent knees. 'That was amazing!' and she hugged Barney.

After that, they all had a go, Barney getting the idea. Not all were so happy with it. Jenny complaining that she didn't like heights, but not wanting to be left out, she managed a circuit. Finally, Ann called them all in praising Barney, and they swamped her with questions.

'Hang on a minute! Ladies, we've forgotten

someone!' Sarah suddenly piped up. 'Mollie!'

Before she could protest, Clare had legged Mollie up and she swung her legs around with a huge grin on her face. They cheered her as she stood up, and she felt literally on top of the world. She sensed his muscles beneath her feet and adjusted. It was the most incredible experience. This was fun! She didn't jump down, but slid to the ground, her knees began shaking.

'Go, Mollie, see you're not so old!!' laughed Clare. Together, they took Barney back to his stable, untacked and fed him. The girls bombarded Ann with questions, until in the end, she ground to a halt with answers.

'Hey, you've all got internet, go research it!' So, for once in the bus, everything went quiet for a while until Jenny exploded.

'Heavens above, these guys are amazing!!'

Mollie itched to see but guessed with a grin, it wasn't practical. Her thoughts flew to Chris, what might he make of all this larking around? She could see that cynical glare that he sometimes had and guessed he wouldn't be impressed. She expected to be abandoned when they got back, but instead found herself being propelled into the sitting room, where they put on the video they had found.

Mollie watched mesmerised. Five girls in skimpy, brightly coloured leotards, hair up in buns like gymnasts, marched into an arena. The horse warmed up - Mollie didn't like how its head was down, over bent she mused. He had a lot of padding around his girth, too. Then the girls ran to him, grabbed the handles and with a bounce from nowhere, leapt on as if it were nothing that he was in canter. The group took turns to leap on and off, but the exercises on the horse were gob smacking. They used the handles and leathers to hold themselves in unbelievable positions. Upside down, in threes with two leaning out in mid-air, pirouettes. All amazing, but Mollie felt her blood go cold at the thought of doing it herself.

'I never imagined that it was like that! You all want to form a team now and do it professionally?'

That had them laughing. 'No, but we will have a go at it!'

'And all in canter.'

'Didn't like how they strapped the horse's face down,' Mollie had to counter.

'But he was beautiful,' laughed Clare. 'Do you think we'll be able to have another go this week?'

'I'm sure Ann has something planned for the next few days!'

Lunchtime was pure heaven to Mollie when at last they included her in their conversation as one of the gang. Clare and Jenny even came with her to walk the dogs, and she discovered a little about them. Such a familiar thing; busy professional parents who sometimes were around, sometimes not. But at least these parents seemed to care a bit, trying to find the most suitable alternatives for when they weren't around in the holidays. The best of everything except time.

The girls saw school as something to be endured; and the church? Mollie got the impression that it was a necessary thing to go there. Ingrained but not argued with or acknowledged as any more than a part of life.

As they came down the fields, Mollie could see the cows mooching near the house, and that Katharina needed milking again. She and Chris had argued about this, he reckoned that eventually the production would equal demand and there would be no problems. He was only too glad to stop the daily grind of milking routine and accused Mollie of being overly sentimental. Perhaps he was right, and she had sort of held on to it, just so she had contact with the cows.

Now she hoped it would be something of a novelty to show the girls. Tonight, she would milk and then maybe get them over being vegans when they tasted fresh milk. The rest of them, even Sarah, were sitting in front of the TV when she got back.

'Right, I've seen one of the cows has got too much milk and I'll need to milk her. Any of you interested?' No response.

'You can have a go at hand milking, or we'll use the machine? Wouldn't you even like to try some fresh milk?'

'EEEWWWWW!' Debbie shrieked. 'Horses I can stand, but cows stink and fart all over the place.' That got a snigger, so Mollie decided to retreat before she could dig herself into an even deeper hole. Back to square one.

It was nice to be back in the dairy; she found cows smelt okay, were warm and companionable. Of course, as soon as the herd saw her going there, they all thought there might be some food in it for them and came down into the yard. It was a struggle to separate Katharina out, but there was a certain satisfaction in giving Ziggy a good slap on the rear and shoving Queenie away from the door. Katharina didn't look that full after all, so Mollie got the stool and bucket.

Katharina stood in her usual place and began munching on the hay. Mollie bent her head into the warm side, crouched and started the rhythmical squeezing down the teats. Despite her sadness at no takers, the day had been good; she had made progress. Katharina swung her head, and Mollie saw Sarah coming in. She stopped and stood up.

'Want a go?'

'Yeah, I've never touched a cow before.'

'She's lovely, one of the friendliest. Let her lick you. She's got a tongue like an old bog brush, but it won't hurt.' Sarah gingerly put her fingers out and let Katharina lick her. At first, she tried to snatch her hand back, but then allowed her. 'That's disgusting! But can I stroke her?'

'She likes it in the dip behind her forelock. She doesn't have horns, so you need not fear her!' Katharina stood there with her eyes shut as Sarah found the right place.

'Now, we must finish milking her. I have this stool to sit on, held on with a belt. Down gently, you might want to wash your hair after this, lean gently into her side. Now grasp a teat at the top, then squeeze the milk downwards with your fingers in order or pull down…that's it!'
Sarah quickly found the best way and the bucket soon filled. 'You have strong hands, are they aching now?'

'A bit! How much longer?'

'I think we're done. Let me take the bucket away so we don't lose it!'

They both stood straight and smiled at each other. Mollie's heart was full. 'We need to let her back out to her calf now, who is going to be furious that there's not so much milk flowing, and she has to work for it!'

'Why don't you milk like on a proper farm?'

As they let Katharina out, Mollie explained her views on leaving calves with their mother and only taking the spare; while at the same time wondering if Sarah matched this to her own life. Mollie was right, the calf butted the near empty udder and Katharina stomped off with a kick.

Back in the parlour, Mollie showed Sarah how she filtered the milk so it could be used. The farm cats, who had appeared from nowhere to have their treat, wove through their legs. They were soon all lapping from a huge saucer.

'Would you like to try it?'

'You know, I would. I'm just following the flow with all this vegan stuff; it means you stay with the in-crowd.'

'I understand what you mean; when I was there, you all had to like Take That!'
Sarah grimaced. 'Things don't change, I don't like Adele…' They laughed, and Mollie found one of the glasses kept for such a moment. They sipped, and she saw Sarah didn't like it.

'It's still too warm for me, but it's so rich, I've never tasted anything like it!' Sarah smiled.

'I'll put some in the fridge. When this has sat for a day, I'll be making butter. I can show you that too.' She washed the glasses.

'Mollie, have you ever considered God and your life?'
Mollie was astonished. Did Sarah have a secret motive to all this? 'Not for a long time; come on, I was at your school too. I was dragged up as a Catholic. I've heard all the arguments. I don't give it a thought these days. But I know you do, why do you ask?'

'I just feel that people should hear it all before they go to hell!'

'Isn't that up to each of us to decide?' Mollie knew this was dodgy ground here.

'But what if you've been fed the wrong or even no information? Hell is a truth if you can understand the spiritual realm.'

This coming from a twelve-year-old? Mollie was now amazed. 'I think we all have the right to believe what we want, but I see your point on the information.'

'I know so strongly that people should know about unconditional love.'

'That's not quite what I was taught.'

'I've read a lot. I have so much time on my hands in school. I read all I can lay my hands on and watch the God channels on the satellite. I'm not sure at times whether I want to stay a Catholic or walk right away from all their rules and regulations that aren't in the Bible.'

'But don't you read what the Popes write and the saints?'

'Oh yes, but they're just people learning from God; the Bible is our handbook.'

'So why the tattoo?'
Sarah looked awkward. 'I was sort of testing myself to find if I can live with such a branding. Seeing what people will say and do to something so open.'

'Sarah, you're twelve. You don't have to decide things yet.'

'I know, but I like some sense of security; a plan that makes the future safe.'
So that was the root of the problem.

'Do you spend much time with your parents? Mine were never around.' Mollie tried changing the subject.

'Oh, we talk now and then on the phone

or the net. They're in the US at the moment. Sometimes I would like to be a nun,' she added randomly.

Mollie tried to keep her mouth shut.

'It seems so secure,' Sarah continued. 'But what use is a good relationship with God if no one else knows about it?'

'I can see what you mean! Do you think he gets bored with all our saying things over and over again?' Mollie smiled, trying things to remain light.

'Oh yes, if I do, surely he must?'

'Have you talked to the priest on this?'

'Oh, I got a load of stuff about being a mother and honouring God that way.' Mollie was shocked.

'Good grief, I imagined the church had moved on from the middle ages these days!'

'I think of it sometimes like a dinosaur when I see what the new churches are doing!' Sarah smiled.

'If you must make a plan, why not talk to God about it?' Mollie felt like she was drowning in this totally new sort of conversation.

'I have, but I don't sense any peace.'

'Then perhaps that's your answer!'

Sarah didn't look too pleased, so Mollie changed the subject.

'Shall we sneak some cake? I've got one in the larder?'

That worked, and they made their way

indoors. There was a lot of giggling and thumping coming from the sitting room. When they opened the door, a heap of girls fell to the floor.

'What on earth?'

After the laughter subsided, Debbie with tears streaming down her face gasped. 'We're trying one of the group movements for the vaulting, if we can't do it on the floor, however, will we do it on Barney?' They were off again. It was catching, even Sarah burst out laughing.

The following days were happier still for Mollie. The vaulting group seemed to work. Sarah got totally involved which Mollie found a relief if it kept her from brooding. They learnt about dismounting over the tail which had Barney nearly bolting the first time.

They all managed walk on his back and even a few strides of trot. This then developed into a lesson of how to jump down off the horse without falling flat on your face. Mollie found an old gym horse on eBay, so they hauled it up to the farm and practised in the barn where the straw gave a softer landing. They tried other horses, but Barney had the widest back and was most accepting of his new role.

Mollie took them out on a ride on their last day and gave them a time they wouldn't forget either. They took the route up the hill to where

Chris had once shown her a round of jumps built into the woods and they steeplechased around that. Then they let the horses paddle in the river and finished up on what was the old race gallops.

She challenged them all to a race. They sort of started in a line, but chaos and bucking broke out before the horses got the idea of being beside each other for a change and took off. Jenny won on Rosy, who despite being sleepy had a hidden turn of speed. In a few days, the girls had softened.

'This is just like a pony book,' remarked Clare as they walked the tired horses home. 'I used to live on them when I first came to school.'
And like in any good pony book, the thought of returning to school caused a little gloom to fall.

'Never mind, you can sign up to come again at Easter, or are your parents around?'

'Mine are still away.'

'Mine too,' echoed three voices.

'Then sign up before anyone else does. And join the gym or get that PE teacher on your side so you can learn the exercises and warm-up routines properly.' Mollie had boned up too on the discipline, and while keeping a distance because she wanted it to be for the girls; she had to be involved.

Her heart overflowed. Things had worked out better than expected and perhaps she would be able to cope with them.

The next holidays were for two weeks and that might change things even more. She wondered what Chris was up to. He would have loved that madcap gallop. They had agreed he would only be in touch if he was on his way back, in this way, he could completely let his ties go.

Even so, she had somehow expected an old school postcard or a text. She now had a few weeks to herself. The foals could arrive and she might play with Amber again. The short week seemed like an age had passed. Then the idea came to her that before Chris had gone, she had talked to him about buying her own horse. Now could be the time.

She had enjoyed riding Amigo, but she actually wanted something with a big stride that ate the miles up, because hacking was her real joy. She had never had a huge competitive spirit; she knew that she didn't have the courage for eventing despite what she said. She patted Amigo's neck, thankful he couldn't read her thoughts.

The next morning was a flurry of packing cases and frantic checking around the house for lost items; along with the realisation that no one had done any homework, but they would have the afternoon to do it. Sister Jo arrived punctually with the minibus, but she still seemed somewhat flustered and non-communicative; very unlike her bossy self. She took Mollie's word that the girls were fine, packed them in and drove away without a further word. Mollie felt a little bereft. Her phone bleeped.

'I've finished the spring sowing, is your

house empty of teenage angst?' Gary seemed to get there before she had time to form the thought. She grinned and sent back a huge thumbs up.

The house seemed very quiet over after the girls had left. Mollie pottered around, tidying up. Joanna and Amber came to visit, and they both found Mollie's tale of woe funny - well Amber simply joined in. They nattered about the weather, then Mollie remembered her plan of buying a horse. This had Joanna digging the local paper out to check out the sales page.

'So, tell me, what is your budget; do you want a kitchen diner and how many bedrooms?' Joanna mimicked the TV shows.

'I'd like something wide and safe, with a good head carriage that doesn't run its nose along the ground and a large, ground-eating stride. I want to hack and explore, not compete.' Mollie was again caught up in a dream picture of herself doing one of the long distance trail rides. This would be such fun.

'15 hand cross TB?'

'Too skitty.'

'Shire cross?'

'But with what?'

'Shetland! No, seriously, might be worth a ring.'

'Are you expecting more visitors?' Joanna

looked out at the front yard.

'No, why?'

'There's what looks like a middle-aged lady dragging a suitcase in our direction!'

Mollie got up to look too and gasped. 'I think it's Sister Jo, and she's not in uniform! What on earth is going on?' Joanna picked up Amber with a giggle. 'I'll leave you with this one, let me know all later!'

She scuttled out the back door, leaving Mollie aghast. More than once she had dealt with unwelcome visitors on her front door, and this was what looked like the worst yet. She quickly shut the dogs in the utility room, which they insisted was a prison, and opened the door. Sister Jo sat on the bench, mopping her brow.

'I'm so sorry for the intrusion, but I had nowhere else to go,' and she burst into tears. Mollie, never one for emotional scenes at the best of times, was flummoxed. She sat down too and waited for the dam burst to stop. She'd never seen a nun cry. They always seemed invulnerable. Should she hug her, or pat her on the arm? Then she remembered her tissues and handed over the packet. That helped; Sister Jo snuffled, snotted and at last dried up.

'I've been waiting for the dispensation from the Holy See, and it arrived yesterday. When I rang the hostel that I had a place in, they said I had lost my room. I couldn't stay at the school, I had to go. It would have been so confusing for the girls.

All of a sudden, I thought of you and wondered if you would take me in as an elderly lost girl?'

Mollie was stumped for words. An ex-nun on her doorstep?

'I will find somewhere. I'm not planting myself on you, just until I get myself sorted out with another place to go.' There was a pleading in her voice that Mollie couldn't refuse.

'Of course, your arrival is a bit of a shock, but, yes, you're totally welcome.' Mollie grabbed the suitcase, which was heavier than bags of feed and led the way indoors and up the stairs. The dogs barked their annoyance.

'Oh, do let them out, I used to love dogs when I was a child.' Mollie took her at her word. They leapt out, stopped, and approached Sister Jo with caution. For once not using their usual knock them over and wash them routine. They sniffed, then lay down in front of her; tummies up in the air for a stroke.

Sister Jo knelt down and caressed. Mollie saw her face had a blissful look, and the dogs squirmed for more attention. There was a threat of tears on Sister Jo's face, but she also seemed as if she was in a trance. Eventually, the dogs got the fidgets, and all three shook themselves and stood up.

'I've never seen a greeting like that!' Mollie had to grin at Sister Jo. 'I think I've lost my dogs!' The moment was broken with the words and they leapt up to wash ears. Mollie went first upstairs and showed Sister Jo the rooms. 'They're not made up, but just say and I'll grab the linen.'

'Oh, this one that has a view over the stable yard and the hill! Give me the sheets. One thing, I'm not Sister Jo anymore. Josephine is the name I took. As I have left the order, I want to be me again. My name is Ruth, although it may take a while to get used to it!'

'No problem, er…Ruth!' Mollie handed over the linen and left Ruth to settle in.

Back in the kitchen, Mollie looked to see what she could offer for lunch, hoping that Ruth wasn't going to be a vegan as well. Before long, she came down to the kitchen, and Mollie handed her a steaming mug of tea.

'I hope you aren't on the vegan thing?'

'No, it's one of these fads of the girls.' She looked close to tears again, but she seemed to pull herself together. 'That bacon smells wonderful!'

Mollie swiftly dished up bacon and eggs. 'Go on, say Grace if you have to!' Ruth did. They ate in comfortable quietness; the dogs sitting, looking adoringly at Ruth, and it wasn't just the bacon. After a large slice of cake, she sat back and began stroking the dogs.

'I owe you an explanation, and I need to tell someone my story. I have to get it out of my system even if I only tell a small part of all. I'm maybe not as old as you think I am, I entered the order very young after following the call, and my life has been a joy. I know I was a bit of a tartar, but so many of you respected me for it, and I'm still in contact with many girls now.

However, on the Easter retreat last year something began to change within me. What had normally been a time to recharge my batteries had me restless and unable to concentrate. I had the strong sensation that there was something inside me trying to wriggle out. It affected everything. I became more short tempered with the girls than normal; even found myself conniving to dodge extra duties and Mass.

That naughty Sarah didn't help either. She's always asking questions, arguing with the priests and us over matters of Holy Doctrine. Then, when Father Ryan confiscated some of the books she read, I found them and read them. Evangelists from the USA, histories of non-Catholic leaders, so many books, they opened up a whole new way of thinking that had the wriggling even worse. That girl is either going to be something great or go totally off the rails!'

'Sarah's quite something, isn't she? When she came to help me with milking, she was trying, if not to convert me, trying to get me to consider God and things that I'm afraid I've walked away from. What happened over the tattoo?'

'What tattoo? Good grief, I must inform…' Ruth caught herself in time and took a deep breath. 'In the end, I told Father Ryan all about it in confession, and after some penance; which I also rushed through. Eventually I talked to him in person.

What he had to say shook me rigid. He said he had been praying for me, and that he felt that I was being told it is time to move on. He stated that it rode against all he believed in and had trained for, but he sensed it deep in his spirit. I had never considered this either, wondering if it was hormones and I should see a doctor. But when he spelt it out, my peace returned along with a huge leap of excitement.

That night I couldn't sleep. Where should I go, what did God want me to do? I looked at all the missionary opportunities, but they seem wrong; I didn't want to join another order. Then it came to me. What I had to do was for want of a better expression, stop being a nun. Leave and let God guide me. That brought back the peace.

While things were set in motion, I kept on looking. They asked me not to inform the girls, as it would be too upsetting. That totally annoyed me, which was also a surprise. It seemed so old fashioned; keep everyone in ignorance; it'll be better this way. They allowed me to tell one other nun, and that got me too. I now itched to leave, although I had no idea where. I was going to take this wonderful leap of faith.

But I had to make some practical steps and finally got a temporary post with an inner-city mission that I thought would give me some time to get my bearings. There were so many delays until all the paperwork arrived yesterday. The hierarchy informed the other nuns. That was so emotional that I very nearly stayed. But no, I had to go. When I rang the mission, my place had been filled due to all the delays. Then I had this picture of your farm, so I got on the bus…'

'That seems almost criminal the way they sent you off.' Mollie looked at Ruth's very worn tracksuit and trainers. 'I guess this is your old P.E. kit? We need to get you some new clothes…and a haircut?' Ruth's hair lay in rough straggly locks, with grey trying to take over.

'I have a little money, some savings from my aunt. We're supposed to hand them over, but I kept them secret; possibly the seeds have been germinating for a long time…but I have to be very careful and make them last as long as possible.'

'Then this is on me! A thank you for all the times you listened to me, even if you had me saying so many rosaries and doing penance to sort me out rather than giving me answers! I have some money from my parents, so no worries, and no board and lodging either. You can help me with the cows!'

That brought a worried expression to Ruth's face, but she didn't argue.

'We'll pop into town this afternoon!' Mollie enjoyed this feeling of turning the tables and being a benefactor. However, she saw dark shadows under Ruth's eyes and that her face was pale. All this must have cost her far more than she was telling.

'One thing, please, not Southampton. I wouldn't want to meet anyone; they all think I'm in London.' She almost pleaded.

'No problem. We can go to Winchester or Bournemouth?'

'Oh, Bournemouth and then we could have a walk along the beach?'

The afternoon was one of pleasure for both women. Mollie had a real buzz being able to pay for all that Ruth wanted. She kept her mouth shut unless asked; knowing that her own colour sense was completely lacking. She had no idea if what Ruth chose worked or not, but perhaps it was just good for her to have what she wanted; regardless of what anyone else thought. Ruth needed everything too. She had found Primark with the girls and so they bought most things there.

Mollie also insisted they visited a better shop and bought a decent coat, shoes and wellies. Ruth kept on thanking Mollie, until in the end she had to tell her the truth about her big pay-off from her parents, who had disowned her for the pure reason they had never wanted her. Mollie didn't like telling it, but she also didn't like this over thankful woman who wasn't her Sister Jo.

They dumped the bags in the Land Rover then walked through the busy streets down to the beach. Mollie watched Ruth looking wide-eyed at the homeless people and some girls on a hen night. Even though it was very early spring, Ruth insisted on taking off her shoes and running along the waves. Mollie cringed inside with embarrassment.

'You know, all those years when I brought the girls on outings, and they leapt around in the sea, I was itching to go but couldn't due to rules. I had to sit, roast and envy. Now I can do what I like!' Ruth grinned from ear to ear.

'Maybe that's what made you so strict with us?' Mollie had a sudden perception of life on the other side, which she was now also experiencing.

'Possibly...I have so much to think through.' Ruth sighed.

Mollie marched her off to a hairdresser. She enjoyed this and, with her hair trimmed into a neat bob, it took years off Ruth. To Mollie, she had become a different person because the penguin outfit had gone. Ruth echoed her thoughts.

'I feel vulnerable. The old habit was safe, people kept their distance. Now I'm just a person. I think I need to go back to your home now.'

When they got back, Ruth gleefully took all her spoils up to her room. Mollie heard and heard her pacing about, slamming doors and cupboards. She guessed Ruth must be having more fun than she had had for years. She took the time to ring Gary, who burst out laughing.

'You are becoming a refuge for lost souls! I hope she's not going to lead you astray and have you Hail Mary-ing and running up the hills singing?'

'Very funny. No, she won't cramp my style, but I have no idea of what I will do with her.'

'Do you have to do anything? Let her be.'

'You're such a well of wisdom. Pub tonight?'

'Yup, but I'm only buying you pints of Holy water.'

Mollie rang off before he could get any worse, but she had a smile on her face. She trotted down to the pub, only to get endless ribbing from Gary, who had only shut up when she said she would get Ruth to tell him all about being a nun.

The new morning heralded a real spring day, Mollie thought of going for a ride, but the mares were all too heavy with foals, so it must be a dog walk. At breakfast, she mooted the idea to Ruth; she probably shouldn't leave her alone in this state, but she also hoped that Ruth might have other ideas. She had gone to her room after supper, refusing the TV.

'I'm not expecting you to entertain me!' Ruth echoed Mollie's inner thoughts. 'I found myself waking at all the old prayer times, I guess that's going to be around for a while. All those years I wanted a lie in…I'd love a dog walk, but I'm completely unfit, so I may not be able to keep up with you.'

'It won't be a hard one. I'll show you around the farm first then we'll go up to the viewpoint, and afterwards to the river. Lunch at the café in the village.'

'That sounds wonderful, something I've never done!' Ruth was soon togged up in her new boots and coat, with her two new doggy disciples thrilled that she was coming too.

Stopping at the gate, they looked up the field. Mollie called to Keith and the mares. He shambled down; his lameness not showing any signs of improving. Mollie knew she needed to get the vet out again.

'Oh, isn't he beautiful!' Ruth didn't see the scars and rough coat. She stretched out her hand and he snuffled her in a friendly way. Then his ears pricked, and he raised his head for one of his imperious neighs.

'He was very close to Chris...I'll tell you the story on the walk.' To her surprise, Keith pushed his forehead to Ruth's chest and rested against her with a soft sigh. They all stood in silence; Keith seemed to be relaxing as he hadn't done for ages. But being him, he suddenly remembered his mares, stood back, turned and galloped up the hill, his tail ever like a banner.

'Animals seem to like you; he's never done that with me before!'

'He's a little sad, possibly missing Chris, as you said.' Mollie didn't get a chance to ask her how she knew that as she was going on. 'I used to have all sorts of pets when I was little, dogs, cats, guinea pigs. I've missed them through the years. Perhaps now I might have a pet again.' she said with a touch of wistfulness. 'Wow, those mares are fat!'

'Foaling's coming soon! I'll have to keep a closer eye on them now. Come and meet the cows and see if they like you too!' Mollie laughed. But the cows were busily munching at the far end of the field, so they left them and walked up the hill. The dogs had great fun, rushing around and jumping in and out of puddles.

'It's no good. I'm too unfit, I need a breather.' Ruth plopped down on the wet grass. 'Look around, this yellow bush blooming, that white over there. I can see the sea in the distance, the oil refinery, and the edge of the forest. Oh, how did He ever think of a spring morning when He began creating in the darkness?'

She turned to the sun and closed her eyes, apparently not expecting an answer. Mollie looked too. She had seen all this so many times; it was quite a revelation to see it with fresh eyes. They were drawn to the farm, which even after a short climb looked like a child's toy.

'Right, I'm okay now!' Ruth took off again with fresh energy. It set the tone for the whole walk, Ruth going in leaps and bounds, exclaiming at some new sight or a flower and then striding off again, but it was in a way huge fun; Mollie having her eyes re-opened. When they got to the café, she told Ruth the story of Chris, his Intersex, the complete story of his attack and healing. Afterwards, Ruth sat back with her eyes shut for a moment.

'Poor, poor man. The old me says that this is something that God had given him so he can learn through his trials. But now I'm not so sure that God would ever want to make us ill.' Mollie was astonished, this really did go against all she had been raised with.

'When will he be returning, I'm looking forward to meeting him?'

'I don't know, we agreed so he was free, but he will ring a day or so before.'

Mollie was relieved. The old Ruth would have given a heavy lecture on sin, sin and more sin. They walked back through the stable yard, Ruth having to peer in each stable and greet each horse. Ann appeared from nowhere.

'I've been trying to call you!'

'There's no signal on the hill.'

'I've had a call from Joanna. Stan found some travellers on the estate and, er, got them to leave. Trouble is, they've left two horses behind. I can't use them. One's a Shetland, Joanna wants that for Amber.' They exchanged grins about an over keen Mum with a four-month-old baby. 'The other is a cob, now I know you're not looking for one. Possibly Chris might like it when he gets back, or you could train it and sell it on, but it needs a home, urgently. The rescue centre near Corfe is full.'

'Mare or gelding? We have to consider his highnesses opinions, or we'll have another disaster.'

'I don't know, but a mare's okay and if it's a gelding you might put him with the cows?'

'You've thought this all through, haven't

you?'

Ann grinned.

'I give in, when do we go and collect them?' sighed Mollie.

'This afternoon?'

'It's almost two already. Let me tell Ruth, I suppose we need my Land Rover?'

Ruth was fascinated when Mollie told her but said that she was exhausted and had to have some quiet time, so to leave her with the dogs. Mollie guessed this might mean a nap.

By the time she got back to the yard, Joanna had arrived. They hitched up the double trailer with copious supplies of halters, ropes, feed and bandages.

'Where's Amber?'

'Driving her dad nuts, she's in crawl mode and keeps taking off. I found her in the kitchen trying to eat the dog food the other day, I'm not disinfecting those bottles anymore!'

It was another world to Mollie and Ann. They caught up on other things as they drove through the village to the field, where Stan waited by the gate.

'How long were they here?' asked Joanna.

'Too flipping long!' laughed Stan.

'They've left a heap of rubbish. I will have to lock all the gates from now on, is that okay?'

'Providing I have a key!' Joanna grimaced as the landowner.

The Shetland was mouse-grey, with an

overgrown mane and long hooves, but friendly and came over to search for treats. They looked at the cob. He stood at the far corner, his back turned; assiduously ignoring them. So, the gate was unpadlocked, and they went in.

Then they stopped in astonishment as he swung around. Obviously young; his quarters were above his withers. His neck was long, and he carried a big head. But the colour! Mollie could hear Ruth in her head, saying that God had used the dregs of the paint pot. He was pink. A roan but with no black markings, just a deeper pink mane and tail. Totally extraordinary. To crown it all, he had blue wall eyes.

Breaking the quiet, Mollie exclaimed, 'No wonder they left him behind!'

The others walked back to get the gear, but Mollie stayed and watched him. They stared at each other. For a second his ears pricked towards her, but then they shot back. He turned and walked away; it was as if he was used to that OMG look from people. Mollie knew she was anthropomorphising things, but she sympathised with him; he was coming home with her.

'How are we going to get him?' Ann had returned with a bucket and halter. Mollie had visions of a cowboy chase around the paddock. She took all the gear from Ann. 'Wait here, let's try the obvious first.' Mollie walked slowly to the right of him so they would come face to face. She kept her body language down and no eye contact. She rustled the feed bucket and walked towards him. She could tell he hadn't moved off. This might be so terrible or so easy.

She saw his hooves through her down turned eyes. Then she was there, and his face shot in to devour the feed. As he filled his mouth and crunched, Mollie got the rope around his neck. With a skill born of years of catching horses, she then slipped the head collar around his head. Slowly, slowly, she lowered the bucket to the ground.

The head collar slipped on and she did up the buckles. Picking up the rope, she lugged him, chomping enthusiastically towards the gate. The others had the ramp lowered; the Shetland loaded. Fortunately, the bucket was well filled, and he didn't bat an eye as he walked up to the ramp. He was too busy eating. Putting the feed down, Mollie backed out carefully and in doing, felt his side. Under the thick winter coat, there was no fat or muscle, just ribs. They raised the ramp as fast as possible and made all secure.

A group sigh of relief went up, and they stowed the gear in the Land Rover. Hell broke loose. There was a one-horse whirlwind in the box. The side was kicked, it rocked like it would turn over. Thunderous neighs and whinnies from a scared Shetland came out the door.

Mollie ran to the front door and, taking a breath entered, a flailing hoof narrowly missing her face. She grabbed another bucket and waved it in the direction of the colt, who was now trying to rear and banging his head doing it. She got the food near his nose and that did the trick. His head dropped, and he munched. How on earth could they get him home if this was what happened each time he emptied it? He would surely get colic.

Then she saw the haynets hung just out of reach. She pulled them over and tied them where he was sure to see them, Talk about the joke of the empty horse. He finished the last mouthful of feed and his ears pricked forward to cause more trouble. She shoved the net towards him. It worked. Munching began. Mollie slipped out and shut the side door with a sigh of relief.

'Let's get home before he finishes the nets!' They waved goodbye to Stan and drove slowly away. 'I can see all my money going on feeding that animal's face,' laughed Mollie.

'He's hungry, and needs worming I expect, he's got to grow a bit yet, and um, a certain little operation!' laughed Ann.

'Oh no, what will I do with Keith? He'll want a punch up.' Mollie remembered earlier fights.

'Actually, an entire colt might be less of a problem than a mare or a gelding. He might have a patriarchal yell at him and then push him out of the herd,' said Ann soothingly, it would not be her problem.

'Well that's no solution, he'd be alone,' worried Mollie. 'Can't he come to you until he has his op, Joanna?'

'I only have a field and I have enough to do with madam. He will need feeding properly, a full vets' check and maybe fitting for some contact lenses.' They all laughed at that. She continued. 'Have you got the cows in the ten-acre?'

'Yes.'

'Well, that's a whole field and two hedges away from Keith.'

'But he'll see. I don't want him jumping out. I know, I'll put the colt in the cows' barn. They can stay out now. It's still deep littered and he can stuff his face from a big bale, while I have a think.' It was agreed.

They arrived at the Manor and drove around the back. The Shetland was no problem, she strode out as if relieved to leave the lunatic. Challenger, Joanna's aged showjumper and his Shetland mate, greeted her with friendship, nickering and nibbling, then they all strode off to inspect the grass together. Joanna rushed off to find Guy and Amber to show them the new arrival.

Much to Mollie's relief, they got to the farm with no further incident. Mollie leapt out into the barn to open a bale of straw which she kicked about over the cows' mess. She cut open a big bale of hay in the corner.

The colt backed out faster than he went in with hay hanging out his mouth. He led easily inside and dived into the bale. Mollie shut the doors with relief, well aware that she hadn't realistically thought the practicalities of horse ownership through properly.

Ann had a brilliant brainwave. 'I'm sure Keith will be okay; you don't want to keep the colt in at this time of the year. Hey, why don't you bring Keith and the mares into the yard for their check-ups, and matey can be in a box and they can meet in a safe way?'

'That might work! I hope he doesn't eat the barn. Have you ever seen an appetite on a horse like that?'

'Never, but he'd eaten all the grass. He's quite big. You know he might make 16 hands when he's finished growing.'

'And that neck!'

'Well, work will help that. You don't have to keep him. In a year's time when he's broken ready to go on, he'll be worth two or three thousand at least!' With that, they arrived at the stables and unhitched the Land Rover. Mollie drove back, wondering what Ruth would make of her strange horse.

The yard was quiet and still when she finally got home. Mollie went indoors in dire need of a cuppa. As the door opened, she was hit with a blast of music coming from the direction of the sitting room. Peering in, she caught a sight that a few weeks ago was unimaginable. There was Ruth jigging and hopping up and down to a music video on the TV. The dogs gave Mollie away, jumping up at her, caught up in the excitement. So, of course,

Ruth saw her and turned bright red and reached for the buttons.

'One of the girls showed me how to use a smart TV, I've had such a wonderful time!' She wasn't embarrassed at all! 'I've found the Tremeloes. I loved them when I was a kid, but I expect they're all either dead or fat and now…' At that, she did seem sad.

'Have you checked them on the net?' Mollie took the buttons, and they both sat on the sofa as Mollie typed in a search. And as expected, they found some elderly and wrinkly men, performing the songs badly. Ruth sighed. 'I think I'd rather remember them as they were…'

Mollie flicked the videos back on. 'Is that better?'

Ruth grinned. 'I don't need to feel my age at all, inside I'm still a kid!' That shook Mollie; if she couldn't reconcile the old and new woman, then Ruth must be having even more trouble.

'Come and see my new horse!' They trudged over to the barn and looked in at the colt who was still stuffing his face.

'I think there's a touch of the chaotic about this fairy creature,' came a soft Irish voice and Mollie looked around in surprise.

'Oh no, that's not coming out as well! I have spent years squashing my accent and the sight of a horse like him has it all pouring out again!'

'I never knew you were even Irish!'

'They frowned on my accent in the school.

There was so much money and upper class accents, I learnt to hide it.'

'Where in Ireland?'

'Cork.'

'Do you have family there still?'

'Maybe a few distanced cousins, but no; I was the youngest and my siblings are long gone.'

'Nephews and nieces?' Ruth appeared uncomfortable at the thought.

Mollie had never expected such depths but left the subject. 'It seems you have caught the name for him!'
Ruth looked askance.

'Chaos completely sums his coat up! Look on his quarters where his new coat is showing, I've never seen such a shade of pink. Did you have horses too?'

'No, but they were always about and I wanted to learn to ride. Being a girl and poor, there was never the chance.' The accent was back under control. 'Yes, it does suit him. I hope he isn't like that in character!' Ruth smiled.

'I'll get the vet out as soon as possible, he needs worming, vaccinations and a thorough check over. That's if he doesn't explode overnight! If he survives, I think he will be huge. Just check how big his cannon bones are!' Mollie could see she had lost Ruth at that point and so they returned to the house.

The following day was Sunday, so Mollie brought up Mass. 'There's a Catholic church in the next village if you want to go.'

'But I've not been to confession...perhaps next week. I'll spend the morning in meditation.' Ruth looked a little embarrassed.

'No problem, but today I'm going to play with my new pony. If you hear blood-curdling shrieks, please call the rescue services!'

Mollie struggled to the barn armed with buckets of feed, grooming equipment and pockets full of treats. Chaos lay flat on the straw and for a moment she thought he had actually killed himself with overeating. But no, an ear flickered, and he turned around and looked at her; his strange eyes making him difficult to read. He sighed and lay back down again. No fear then!

She went in and he still didn't get up. Now her alarm bells were going off; she was going through all the digestive problems she knew. He picked his head up again as she approached, then with the speed of the young horse he stretched his feet out and lurched up. Mollie stood as he gave himself a thorough shake, winter coat exploding into the air.

'Chaos, here we are. Will we be friends?' She had a treat in her hand and stretched it out to him. Two very pink lips flapped and took the treat which disappeared with hardly a crunch, and he was nosing her for more. She gave in and fed him several, but he mustn't use her as a feed dispenser.

'I think that's enough for now!' She took him by the halter, he sighed and followed her. So, he was at least halter broken. He tied to the side like an old pony and she began grooming him. His hair was not only thick, but it was also matted; she'd never seen the like of it. Not wanting to push anything, as he was such an unknown, Mollie worked thoroughly over his coat.

His long mane made Mollie remember a Facebook picture of one of those horses with manes and tails trailing along the ground and grimaced to herself. She found the itchy spots on his shoulders and gave him a good hard scratch. As she had hoped, his face began to quiver, his lips puckered, and he dropped his head to her shoulder and began grooming her in return. He didn't try to bite. He nuzzled hard, all showing a gentle character; much to Mollie's relief. She slowed down and let him be.

Now to try his hooves. She ran a hand down the hairy legs, but they stayed planted. Same with each leg, but Mollie had all the time in the world. She wanted to make friends with him today, not to start the training. She parted the hair to see what his feet were like. Soup plates, white with black stripes and very overgrown that must be dealt with soon. She ran her hands all over, he was unbothered, he must have been fairly well treated by the gypsies. Why had they left him, would they want him back? Perhaps she needed to set something out in writing about this?

Chaos got bored, and as he hadn't eaten for a while, he barged past her and shoved to make his way to the hay. Mollie asked him to stop with a low voice, and he did with a touch of surprise.

'With your size, you're not going to walk all over me!' She couldn't read those eyes. The blue colour seemed to take all the usual expression out of them. Outside came a yell from Keith. Perhaps he had seen another horse on the hill, but the effect was that Chaos jumped and tried to turn to the window. Mollie wrestled with him, this was a point she had to make, and she won. Although he continued trying to turn towards the sound, she got his attention and rewarded him. Thankfully, Keith piped down.

What now? She really wanted to put Chaos out, but as he looked at his big bale, she let him go for now. Vet call first thing in the morning.

Ruth was ensconced in her room, so she took the dogs and walked over to Gary's farm. It was almost a relief to leave. She had no idea of how she should deal with Ruth. She couldn't think of anything in common to talk about. How long would she be stuck with her? She poured this all out into his sympathetic ear.

'Well, get proactive in finding her a new place? Do nuns get a pension? Is it possible for her to rent somewhere?' he suggested.

'No idea on the pensions, but she did say she had a bit of money,' Mollie pondered.

'Well, don't let her hang around, get her on that PC and phone!'

'I feel mean. She did sort of watch out for

me at school in her bossy way,' she sighed. 'But that is a good idea. Why didn't I think of it? You're such a fount of wisdom, Gary!'

'I know, I'm such a star! How are you going to thank me…?'

It was a another beautiful spring morning and Mollie waited for the arrival of the vet. Ruth had been quiet at breakfast, so Mollie didn't want to make her unhappier. If she was working out major stuff in her head, then she needed some space and not others' ideas. Chaos still ate as if it would run out, and she wanted to get him on some fresh grass. The vet's van turned into the yard, so she went to catch Chaos.

'Well, he's really something else, what a colour! Heavens knows what I'll write on his passport.' Mac knew Mollie and Chris well. 'Let's check his teeth… He's got his tusks, so he's not such a baby. You can start breaking him in with no doubts. He might have a growth spurt when you improve his nutrition, so don't rush into new saddles!' Of course, Mac lifted Chaos's feet without a problem.

'Had me caught me on that yesterday, had them concreted to the floor!'

'Oh, he's going to be a bright one too. I pulled his feathers, perhaps that's what he's used to. You're lucky that he doesn't seem to have been ill-treated in any way.' Mac ran his hands along Chaos's back. 'We need to see him move.'

'Slight problem there, Keith.'

'They'll have to meet sometime.'

'I guess I'm simply worried about him doing something else idiotic!'

'Why don't you get them in, Keith's due for a check over, and the mares too. Let them shout at each other over a door. While you're catching them, I'll fill him with vaccination and worm him.'

'Someone else has already suggested that idea. I'll fetch them.'

Mollie walked to the field gate and whistled through her fingers. From nowhere came Keith's answer, and she gloried in his beauty as he cantered down the hill. The mares were with him, which would save her a trip. The three thundered into the yard and came to the barn, where they were usually stabled. Mollie threw some hay down and moved to halter them, but Mac stopped her. 'Wait for it!'

A pink explosion tried to get out over the barn stable door, which was fortunately old and sturdy. Mac and Mollie held their breath. But Keith, as ever not running to course, leant over to the door with a friendly knicker and the two exchanged snorts and mini bites.

'He's an old softy, really!' laughed Mollie in relief.

The mares came over too but were far grumpier; telling the funny looking thing that they were the real bosses. Mollie tied them up and Mac looked quickly at Keith's scars while he was diverted.

'This scar has healed up rapidly since I last saw him. Don't worry any more on his lameness. He needs to move more, so having a playmate will do him good.'

Mac looked at the mares' udders. 'They're bagging up nicely. I think it may be a good idea to put them in a field away from Keith. He can be a bit unpredictable at best,' he said straightening up. 'It could work in your favour having this roseate object here, turn him out with Keith and it might stop him missing them. There's plenty of grass in that hill field.'

'If I put the mares in the orchard, that's right by the house,' said Mollie thoughtfully. 'They need some work on their coats too...Will you hang on for a few minutes in case there are any problems?'

'Of course, it's more than my life's worth to have dramas with Keith, and Diane will pay for the extra time!'

They put Keith back out, and before he realised, the girls weren't there, put the mares into the orchard. Then came the interesting bit. Chaos was more than ready to stretch his legs and would have barged Mollie through the door, so she turned him each time he tried to rush until he calmed down and let her out first. Mac led the way as Chaos bounced his way to the gate, but he wasn't out of control; simply happy.

Keith stood up on the hill, looking for his girls so they had time to release Chaos and shut the gate firmly. He stood there for a moment, then whipped around and hurtled up the field, not having seen Keith, pure joy showing in his every movement. With his scraggy tail in the air and a huge buck, he saw Keith and trotted over to say hello. Mollie and Mac held their breath.

The two horses stood nose to nose and proceeded to squeal at each other. They began mock striking, then nipping. As a couple, they suddenly took off at a gallop, side by side careering around the field like two excited foals; squealing and bucking. They careered past, matched like a pair of carriage horses, paying no attention to Mollie and Mac whatsoever. They started to slow and soon their attention turned to the fresh grass.

'I think they'll be fine, as Chaos is entire, he's a buddy.'

'Keith used to beat the seven bells out of a gelding if we tried to turn one out with him.'

'That was another situation entirely. Chaos turned up at the right time. But keep an eye on them for this first day or so. I don't see any real problems occurring. As soon as the first mares arrive for service, we'll haul Chaos out and he can have his little operation! When do they start arriving?'

'Chris said straight after Easter. Diane hasn't booked in so many this year and they're coming straight here.' Mollie remembered last year and Liz the tyrant who ran the stables, who had made her drive all the mares up the hill, causing a lot of extra work.

'All sounds good. Any problems, I'll be here!' Mac gave a cheerful wave. Mollie wanted to find Ruth and tell her all the news. She was in her room again, so Mollie barged in without really thinking about it. Ruth was curled up in a ball, sobbing.

'Hey, what's the matter?' Mollie sat down beside her.

'I've made such a huge mistake. I'm missing the girls and I can't see the future. I don't know what to do next.'

'Well, I guess it must be a major shock for you. Do you want to go to Mass? I can drive you over to the next village?' Mollie asked again as she couldn't think of anything else.

'As if that would help. I'd get millions of prayers to say. I'm sure God gets as bored with them as I do!' Ruth exclaimed bitterly. 'No, just leave me. I mustn't inflict myself on you anymore.'

'But you are here with me and I want to help.'

'Oh, leave me alone!' The snappish voice was more like a certain nun. 'I helped you out with getting the girls here. You don't appreciate how much officialdom and paperwork and regulations I saved you by contacting the parents directly for you. There are rules for boarding girls in this day and age. You owe me nothing, give me some space!' Ruth looked aghast at what she had said.

But Mollie had had an idea; she was used to being told off by Sister Jo. 'I'm going to make a phone call.' Five minutes later, she returned.

'You say God doesn't organise things? I called Joanna at the Manor. Now, let me get this right... Joanna's dad is married to Diane, who was Joanna's best friend. Dianne's mum, Chloe, who I think is an honorary aunt, is the most wonderful Christian lady.

She does lots of churchy things and is renowned for her hugging abilities. She's here at the moment, so we're going over to meet her. I'm sure she'll have some ideas for you, even if she's not Catholic!'

Ruth looked up, not altogether sure. 'I'll try anything now, but can we go in the car? I really don't feel fit enough to walk over that hill again!'

Mollie regretted everything as they drove over. Ruth had gone very quiet and answered in monosyllables when she told her about the horses. They went straight into the kitchen where Joanna, Amber and Chloe sat at the kitchen table.

Chloe got up straight away and engulfed Mollie in a hug. She felt something lifting from her as she always did. But Chloe looked tired when she pulled away, her long blonde hair looked dull and her clothes not as immaculate as usual.

'What's up with you?' Mollie blurted.

'James, he's disappeared again right after

he had left rehab. But that's his problem. He knows where I am. Is this Ruth?' She strode over to where Ruth looked as if she wanted to disappear into the ground.

'Dear Ruth, we have so much to talk about!' A straight-backed Ruth was pulled into a full embrace, and Mollie saw her relax. Chloe kept her arm around her and whisked her out of the room without a word; leaving Mollie with her Goddaughter and Joanna. At least they were interested in the next episodes of the adventures of Keith.

Ruth refused to tell Mollie anything on what she and Chloe had discussed when she was dropped back later that afternoon and apologised for her outburst. She seemed more at peace. Mollie was giving the mares a groom, as they looked a little bedraggled as their winter coats were coming out in lumps.

'Give me a hand? I haven't started on Dixie yet?' Ruth gave her a shy smile and watched as Mollie showed her how to use the metal curry comb.

'Thanks for introducing me to Chloe. She's going to do some ringing around for me and might be able to find a place for me if I don't insist on it being Catholic!'

'See, I told you!' It suddenly struck Mollie at how she found it easy to pile out Godly advice to other people but wouldn't talk to him personally at all. She shelved the idea. The hair flew in the air as the two worked. Dixie almost smirked under Ruth's touch, her eyes half closed and every muscle enjoying the sensation. Ruth was oblivious, deeply in thought.

'Her stomach moved!' she shrieked in panic and dropped the curry comb. Mollie showed her how the foal was lying and how soon it might be born. Now Ruth was fascinated, and they had a full on conversation about horses foaling and all that it entailed.

The following weeks were peaceful ones. Ruth seemed to have put her sorrow behind her. She invested in a mobile phone and talked a lot to Chloe. She helped with the horses and even got to know the cows, but she didn't like them as much as the horses. The dogs were her constant shadows. Mollie felt a bit jealous. Ruth still had the Tremeloes on full blast when she thought Mollie wasn't around, so Mollie had showed her how to listen on her phone. Keith and Chaos remained good buddies.

Both mares produced little images of themselves, not Keith coloured, and much earlier than expected. It was a joy watching them playing together in the orchard. Chaos was growing. Mollie watched him fill out day by day. His quarters lay more in line with his withers, his neck thickening out. In his summer coat he looked even more startling than before.

She decided to leave breaking him in until after his operation and the girls had gone home after Easter. She was surprised when she had a couple of messages from them, telling her that they had new gym classes where they could practice and how they looked forward to being with her again. It meant so much to her, Ruth understood.

Finding somewhere for Ruth was taking its time, as many places had waiting lists or needed some form of proof of income or pension. Chloe was putting a lot of work into it, which Mollie could see displaced her worry about James. It seemed a drug addict never healed.

Then Mollie found the solution. When she was looking for the bookings for the visiting mares, she switched on Chris's PC to check his database as she couldn't find the file anywhere. She saw the web page of where he had gone to in Dorset. It looked like they specifically took on people in dire straits like Ruth.

She copied down the details and made Ruth email this Eustace who ran the organisation. Bingo! They had a place, and so a week before the girls were due to arrive, Ruth got ready to leave. To Mollie's surprise, she came down the stairs once more as Sister Jo.

'Don't say anything. I'm not a nun anymore. I kept this when I left. It's totally irrational, but I feel safer. I've got my bus times, and a taxi booked to take me to the centre. Thank you, Mollie, heavens knows where I would be if you hadn't taken me in. I don't know if there will be internet there, but if not, I'll write you some good old-fashioned letters!'

For the first and maybe last time in her life, Mollie was hugged by a nun who had been a teacher. Ruth insisted that she walked into the village and so she left, Mollie watching her go with a mixture of relief and sadness. Ruth also had a letter with her for Chris, for there had been no word from him. They had agreed with this, but somehow she had expected him to be in touch.

Never mind, the girls returned soon. She might enjoy some time alone and Gary could now pop in whenever he wanted. He hadn't taken to Ruth. He said it was her inherent cleanliness and churchiness that he didn't like.

Sitting once again on the front doorstep with a cup of coffee before she went to clean Ruth's bedroom, Mollie heard a vehicle coming up the lane and idly wondered if it was a delivery. But no, around the corner came Chris's truck and Chris in it. The dogs took off with a peal of barking. They knew it too and were looking for their mate Rex. Chris stopped in a flourish of dust and piled out of the truck.

'MOLLIE!' They hugged like two happy bears, then pulled back to look at each other. Chris was tanned and had put on weight. He wasn't fat but had filled out from his usual skeletal form.

'You're great! I've been wondering about you so much, and there's loads to tell you! Where's Rex?'

'Likewise! He fell in love with a cocker spaniel, so he has moved in with Alan. Let me get my things while you put the kettle on!'

Mollie skipped like a foal into the house and rummaged around for some cake. Chris thundered upstairs to dump his bags, and at that moment the doorbell rang. It looked like it was a day of surprises. As Mollie opened the door, she was glad that she didn't suffer from a heart condition. Looking thin and tired, with bags showing under her highly made-up eyes, stood her mother.

'You father passed away a few weeks ago, so I thought I would pay you a visit.' Mollie's mother shouldered her way past the astonished Mollie and dumped her bags on the floor. The dogs rushed out to greet one of their friends and wanted to jump up at her.

'Get those beasts off me and get them under control.' Her mother barked.
Something rose, in Mollie, a wave of anger and strength that she had never experienced before.

'No, I will not. This is my house. I can do what I want in it. You are not invited. You are not legally allowed to be here. If you think you can march in here and start off like before, you're mistaken. This house is on my terms.' Mollie registered to her inner horror that she had stood up to her mother. She had also almost said she could stay.

Her mother, for a split second looked her straight in the eyes with an expression that Mollie didn't understand, then fell to the ground in a dead faint.

CHAOS

Mollie looked for a minute in a state of complete shock. At the same moment, Chris came thundering back down the stairs. He ground to a halt and looked in horror as well at the fallen woman.

'What on earth has happened here? Who is she?'

'I'm afraid this is my mother. I don't know why she's turned up. We better do something, we can't leave her lying here. The dogs will be licking her all the time!' Mollie tried to make light of the situation in an effort to hide her anger. Together, they picked her up. Mollie was appalled at her mother's gaunt frame. Under her clothes, she was all bones and weighed nothing. Mollie could have carried her on her own. They got her into the sitting room and laid her on her side on the sofa. Mollie's first aid training had kicked in.

Molly and Chris looked at each other for a second. They both remembered the time when Chris was so injured that he had to be carried onto the sofa, too. Molly's mother remained away from the world; completely out cold. They both wondered what to do with her. In the end, Molly fetched an old blanket from the cupboard, and they covered her over.

'Why on earth has she turned up here?' moaned Mollie. 'I've got the lost girls here in a week. She can't stay! Do you think we need to get a doctor?' Guilt suddenly engulfed her. A snore came from the sofa as if in an answer and at that moment, Mollie caught a whiff of alcohol. Her mother was drunk. In disgust, she spun around and returned to the kitchen. Over mugs of tea, the two friends spent a good couple of hours catching up on what had been happening.

'What is Sue up to now?'

'I stayed in Swanage for a while after we celebrated her 18th birthday. After we recovered, she took off to various places for her coaching tests for the Riding for the Disabled Association. After that, she will to move into the flat at the stables. Once she was 18, all help from the Social Services ended. I will be going back to Swanage as I've got a summer job!'

'Doing what?'

'Working in a fish and chip shop on the seafront!'

'YOU? COOKING?'

'Well, it's not that complicated. I have to get some hygiene certificate. Once that's done, I'll be mostly prepping and serving at tables.'

'Where will you live?'

'I'm not returning to Alan, if that's what you mean. It would be convenient if I want to meet

Sue, but I believe my time there is over. I've got a shared flat above the shop.'

'I can't see you doing this! But then again, who would have thought I'd be feeding vegan food to teenagers?' Mollie filled their cups again. 'I'm going to be nosey here. Did you go and get yourself sorted out at the doctors?'

'No, when all the plans went awry, I decided to wait. Alan was right. I needed to sort me out first and the rest might be better left until I was more complete.' Mollie saw he was squirming a bit, so changed the subject. Yet she picked up another proverbial shovel. 'So, is there something going on with Sue?'

Chris stiffened. 'No, we simply clicked. It's not like us. Sue and I were thrown together and we get on. She's only a kid and pretty mixed up herself. Won't talk about her home and what got her convicted. No, she's a mate, like you, but a younger model!' He grinned rakishly at her. Mollie left it at that, she knew when to stop pushing.

'And you and Gary? Mollie, you're blushing! I've never seen you do that!'

Now she squirmed. 'We meet and go out and it's good. He doesn't put me under any pressure. Chloe has been around.' She changed the subject as quickly as possible. 'James has disappeared, and no one can find him. I think helping with Ruth has distracted her'.

'Shall we check on the old bat? I'd like to check my animals.' Chris didn't pursue things either. A gentle snore came from the sitting room. Quietly, they slunk out with a mutual sense of relief.

The cows were grazing near the gate and Chris greeted them. They remembered his voice; licking and trying to shove him about.

'I guess you're not milking?'

'Okay, you were right!' laughed Mollie. 'They did all calm down after a while and adapt to what milk was being taken. Even when the spring grass came through, too. The AI man's been out a couple of times. I got them in the crate and wrote it all down as you said. But we have to find a long term plan on what you plan to do with them. When do you want to send the bullocks on...' Mollie gulped. She liked her roast but wasn't so good with the technicalities of it all.

'I'll have a chat with Gary. Between us we'll come up with a plan for both the herds in autumn. Will that do?' said Chris.

Mollie smiled with relief; while she enjoyed the milking side, she didn't like this side of farming life so much. They turned and walked to the field where Keith grazed.

Chris stopped. 'What the dickens is that?' He watched Chaos and Keith mock fighting under the trees. Mollie hastily told him the whole tale; making sure he was happy and knew that Mac had approved the scheme.

'Well, I suppose that's all right. The buck stops with me as far as Keith and Diane are concerned, but they appear happy. But good grief, that horse has a crazy colour scheme!' Chris was secretly a bit miffed as he had expected Keith to come rushing up to him, like a long-lost friend.

'Mac reckons it's because Chaos is entire that Keith has accepted him rather than beating him up.'

'So where are the mares?'

'In the orchard. Two lovely bay fillies. Yes, I kept them away from Keith when they came into foaling heat as you ordered.'

The mares came over with their babies, who stayed cautiously behind, peering at the new person. Mouse and Emma remembered their owner and frisked Chris for goodies.

'What will you do with them now?' Mollie hoped some indirect questions might reveal what Chris was planning long term; their agreement only ran until Christmas.

'I'm not sure, I might send them to Eustace's stables as they are a bit wasted here. Perhaps Sue could break the foals in later. No rush to decide, is there?'

'None at all. It's also been arranged that when the first Keith mares arrive, Chaos will come in and have his operation. Following that he can go out with the mares. That okay?'

'Sounds well planned out, it's good to come back and find only one form of chaos here. I'll talk to the contractor about the hay later, then I can tell you which fields to close.' His phone rang. 'Oh, hi

Sue, how'd the test go?'

There was a new note in his voice that Mollie hadn't heard before. She felt a pang of jealousy. In an excuse not to overhear or investigate her feelings, she returned in to check her mother.

She was still out of it, so Mollie nipped upstairs and made up a spare bed. She had a real sense of doom on this. At least Chris didn't mind her being here. The idea of dealing with this bag of emotions on her own didn't bear thinking about.

Chris disappeared for ages. She guessed he was walking the fields like a true farmer. Not wanting to wake her mother, she got on with making a beef stew for the evening. The dogs helped, devouring the spare bits and sat, looking lovingly at the dish.

'I wouldn't let dogs in my kitchen. It's most unhygienic.'

'Oh, how are you mother? Did you have a nice nap?' Well dodged, thought Mollie.

'Yes, the journey was most tiring.' Her mother dodged the issue too. Could she be unaware she had passed out?

'Cup of tea?'

'Lovely, Earl Grey, with a touch of lemon.'

Fortunately, one of the girls had left a packet. Mollie wasn't going to do the best china bit; mug or nothing here. She watched the look on her mother's face when she was handed the tea, but she didn't comment and sipped in silence.

'I'm doing a stew for supper. Mash or rice with it?'

'Rice is fine. Have you got a nice bottle of red to go with it?'

'I'll see later.' This got Mollie's anger rising enough to get her to sit at the table and take her mother to task.

'So, what brings you here?'

'I wanted to tell you in person about your father.'

'Why, when you didn't even tell me in time for the funeral?'

'There was so much red tape and with dear John taking over the part directorship, things got fairly out of hand.' Did her mother say that she actually grieved?

'What happened?'

'He keeled over during a board meeting. Nothing could be done. We tried everything, but even with a heart-starting machine that was in the building, nothing worked. We're such a go-ahead business.'

'Are you going to take over some of his work?'

Mollie's mother's lip curled. 'No, I don't do golf and poker.'

'But surely he did a lot more than that?'

'Not really, he was just a figurehead. John has run things for quite a long time.'

Mollie remembered their pet director. He had struck her as no fool, even though he had been lied to about her. Her parents had told him, that Mollie was in a care home. She had seen a twinkle in his eye though and guessed he was no one's stooge.

'Are you going to retire now?' Mollie realised she had no idea of her mother's age. Her thick makeup and dyed hair meant she might be anywhere between 50 and 70.

'I may take it easier or I might try something new.'

'Like?'

'I may go on a cruise or take a trip to the Scottish estate.'

'What estate?'

'Oh, it belonged to your father. We had it done up a few years ago and converted the castle into a hotel.' Mollie knew she was sitting with her mouth open, so she snapped it shut. She had never known how much her parents were worth. No wonder they had the money to pay her off. That reminded her.

'What about the legal agreement that we were no longer to have any contact with each other? You effectively cut me off. How do you think you can simply roll up here and expect me to let you in?'

Her mother didn't reply, but looked at her without any form of response. A blank stare that said nothing; as if Mollie's words meant nothing to her. Finally, she mumbled. 'I came to tell you as a matter of courtesy.'

'YOU! A matter of courtesy? You never wanted me! You got me out of the house as quickly as possible. It was no fun being the only five-year-old in that boarding school. You topped it off by paying me off and made it clear you don't want me. Now you turn up here and expect to stay?'

Again, that blank stare. They glared each other out and were saved by the arrival of Chris.

'Oh, hello, I see you've slept off the booze,' he said curtly. He seemed equally wound up by something; but bless him for the bluntness.

'It was nothing but tiredness and a little drink on an empty stomach.' She smiled rakishly at him. 'I wanted to pop in and tell Mollie the sad news. It's such a shame she missed the funeral.' Mollie' jaw was dropped again.

'Who?'

'Only her father,' Mollie's mother dismissed.

Chris was as shocked as Mollie. Unable to reply, he turned to make himself a cuppa.

'It was so kind of you to take Mollie in. I hope she hasn't been too much trouble.' Did she even know what she was saying?

Chris snorted. 'If that is what you think, then you are seriously deluded.' Chris's turn to get that look.

'Let's eat.' Mollie suggested in desperation. She dished up. Her mother remained silent.

'Did you find that wine we were talking about?' She suddenly demanded in her old, forceful manner.

'Er, no, I'll have a look.' Mollie returned with a bottle of supermarket best and poured a small glass. Her courage began to desert her.

'Oh, don't be mean!' Mollie filled it up without comment.

They ate the meal in silence. Mollie saw that her mother drank lots and pushed the food around her plate, pretending to eat. At last, the ordeal was over. Her mother had downed two large glasses, and she had a real glow on her cheeks.

'That was so delicious! I'm still quite tired from all the travelling. I'll have an early night. Which room have you made up for me?' With as few words as possible, Mollie showed her in. As she was about to slam the door, her mother looked straight at her.

'He's not the type for you. He's a man's man. You're wasting your time.' Mollie turned and ran back downstairs.

'If it didn't scare me, I would like a glass myself. Chris, what am I going to do with her? She's completely nosey, nasty and irritating.' Mollie wailed.

'Something's wrong with her. Maybe a breakdown?'

'No, she's a bloody-minded old drunk?'

'No, she's after something. A plea for help she can't express.'

'This is all very profound from you, Chris.' Mollie stared at him in surprise.

'Staying with Chris and Sam and their love for people makes you soften. You find things in people and then, where once we would have condemned, forgive and love. Don't forget she's recently lost her husband. Whatever that stands for, it's still a shock.' Chris seemed more reasonable and caring than he had ever been before.

Later that night, Chris lay in his old attic bedroom, back in that familiar dip in the mattress. The old house creaked itself down to rest. In some respects, nothing had changed. He almost believed that in a couple of hours, he would hear his father rumble down the stairs, swear at the dogs and go out to milk.

He swung back into the present, where so much had changed. Mollie was still his dear friend, but they both now had new things in their lives to deal with. He was glad that it wasn't his mother lying in that state downstairs.

Thoughts of Sue and the new life he had planned for the summer had him fighting sleep. He tossed and turned through the night hours, unable to make any sense of it all. There was something else as well. It nagged away at the back of his mind. It all seemed to have started when Keith hadn't rushed over to him with that familiar knicker.

This triggered a sort of pain inside. His

thoughts led to remembering the time following the attack. Echoes of the negativity and depression that struck him down as his body healed. Being back in this house was oppressive. He'd never felt this before; it had been home.

It became clear. The thought of being tied down to the farming year, even Keith, all his childhood memories that were in every corner. They all combined to thwart and repress him. How would he be able to put all this past stuff behind him when he came back for good? That was it; he had returned to being trapped and caught here. With that sorted, he finally found some peace and rolled over to sleep.

Mollie woke early the next morning and pottered around tidying up. She didn't dare go and check on her mother; she had a fear that she might have choked and died in the night.

The dogs, who had kept well away from her mother, jumped about asking for a walk. She was tempted, but didn't want to go too far away. To her relief, Chris stumbled down the stairs, looking as if he had slept badly too.

'Remind me to buy a new mattress, my back's really aching!' He grinned and rumpled his hair. 'I need some fresh air, shall I take the dogs up the hill for you? They've got the want out look about them.'

'Please do. I must stay here. I'm worried about my mother.'

'Oh, she's still asleep. I heard snoring! I may go and visit Joanna and Chloe afterwards. Catch up with them. There's nothing planned for today?'

Mollie wanted to say please don't leave me alone with her, but he looked like he needed to be away too.

'Go on, I'll deal with the beast when it emerges!' she grinned. Chris and the dogs were gone in an instant. She watched them in the yard, hearing Chris's sheep whistle calling them along. Keith came down the hill, Chaos not recognising the call. She saw horse and man greeting each other; Keith bowing his head and nibbling at Chris's hair. The bond seemed as strong as ever, but after a while, Chris gave Keith a slap on the neck, who turned and galloped back up to the hedge line and Chaos.

A large black car entered the yard, and Mollie went out to greet the visitor. A tall, familiar looking man in a grey business suit got out and looked around. Seeing her, he smiled, and she remembered. It was John, the CEO of her parents' business. He held out his hand. 'Is she here?'

'Yes, she came in and collapsed on me yesterday. What's going on John?'

They stood in the yard, both unwilling to go in. 'You weren't at the funeral.' He scowled at her.

'I didn't know anything about it until

yesterday. I am officially divorced from them, or had you forgotten that?'

'Myra insisted that she had told you. I guess it's all part of the problem.' He sighed.

Mollie wouldn't budge; she wasn't going to be wrong-footed. She waited for more.

He carried on at last. 'At the board meeting after the funeral, things turned pear-shaped. We all tacitly understood that she drank but ignored it. She arrived looking, well, not her usual self. She proceeded to contradict things that had been arranged and refused to sign documents that Peter had left to be sorted out.

In the middle of the argument, she passed out. We took a decision to get her admitted to a small clinic nearby and for a while she was fine. When they took her off the knockout pills, she did a runner. This is the only place we could think that she might come to after we checked all the houses and the hotel. She needs to go into some form of rehab.'

'And who says you are the one to decide?'

'Well, it isn't you.' That stung. But he was right.

'Take her away. Last night, all she mumbled about was putting things right in between criticising us and then going off on some random train of thought. She arrived here reeking of booze and there's no fat on her; it was like lifting skeleton.'

At this, John appeared to relax a bit. 'I was

worried that you had bumped her off or vice versa.'
He nearly smiled.

'Things were never that bad!' Mollie began
to raise her voice in shock. 'What has been said
about me?'

'Calm down.' To her relief, she saw that
twinkle back in his eye. 'I have a fair idea of what
she's like.'

Now they walked indoors and found
Mollie's mother sitting at the kitchen table. Mollie
was so tempted to call her Myra; she'd never
known her name. Her mother had a cup of tea,
presumably from the pot in front of her, but it
looked an odd shade of brown.

'What are you doing here, John? I
understood we had dealt with all the documents.
Now you disturb this time with my daughter.' She
was angry, tapping a spoon against the cup.

'I wondered why you'd left the hotel you
were staying in. I decided I'd pop by to see what
you are up to.'

'Oh, I'm just helping Mollie get her life in
order. She's so out of control in her relationships;
such unsuitable men.' She glared a smile at him.

'Mother, you arrived here yesterday
afternoon and passed out on us. When you did
come around, you drank nearly a whole bottle of
wine. After that, you took off to bed. At 7 pm.'

'Nonsense, the tiredness got the better of
me. I've been through a lot. I am a grieving widow,
you know. More than I can say for you; not a

tear for the loss of your father!' The nastiness had returned.

'You are deceiving yourself. Mother, you are an alcoholic and you need treatment. You are going with John to rehab to get yourself sorted out.'

'I've never heard such nonsense in my life. I know when I'm not wanted. I will pack my case and leave. Call a taxi.'

To Mollie and John's huge relief, she passed out again. Mollie checked the more than half-drunk cup. She found it was mostly whiskey. Where had she discovered that?

'I'll get her stuff. Then we'll carry her out.' Mollie ordered crisply, unconsciously echoing her mother's better days. John didn't argue. Once they had her on the back seat, wrapped in a blanket, Mollie's wrath and courage slipped.

'Divorce or not, will you keep me informed of how she is? Will the business be okay?'

'Peter sorted it all out. He had been told that he didn't have long and stitched it all up. Don't worry, I won't be making off with the family silver. I've got her booked into a really good clinic on the outskirts of Basingstoke like the Betty Ford ones. Give me your mobile number.'

That done, he drove off as if late for an appointment. Mollie began to shake like a leaf. She went into the kitchen and nearly drank her mother's tea. In fury, she threw it against the wall. For the first time in her life, she cried for her parentless childhood.

'Oh, honey, what's happened?' From nowhere, Chloe had arrived and engulfed Mollie in one of her famous hugs that put the now right, if not the past.

After a few tissues, Mollie pulled herself together and looked at Chloe properly. She wasn't looking that good either. She looked dull and unkempt; not her usual effervescent self.

'Chloe, what's happened?'

'I've found James. He's hanging out in Winchester with some of his old school cronies.'

Mollie looked askance.

'I've been naughty. I used a private detective when he left rehab. I expected a call to pick him up, but nothing. I'd only seen him the week before and we were planning a trip away. He was off everything this time, even had an idea for a new book. A huge settlement for the film rights on another is in the pipeline. I think that's what tripped him off to go and party. Like he's done so many times before, as you well know.'

Mollie grimaced; she had no time for James. He had used her and caused all sorts of problems before he had met Chloe. She had a sudden realisation. 'You want me to come with you to find him?'

Chloe nodded. 'You understand what I'm going through and none of the others could come,' she smiled sorrowfully. 'I don't like asking for help, but I am at an endpoint and I need someone to support me, whatever the outcome.'

'Of course, I'll come. Chris is out with the dogs, and there's nothing much to do here. Who's driving?'

They drove carefully down the narrow streets of the older part of Winchester and eventually parked near the College. Mollie was glad they had brought the mini. She didn't think her Land Rover would have liked the squeeze. Chloe pulled the key out and sat back.

'As you're not a believer, please understand I need to pray about this. Will you find a way to agree with me?'

Mollie nodded.

'Lord, help. Help me to say the right words that you would have said. Don't let my anger run away with me unless it is your anger too. Holy Spirit, please guide my tongue. I don't know any more if this relationship is your plan for me. I can no longer tell if it is right, or even why we shared that deep spiritual connection at first. Help both James and me. Help me find your resolution so I will once again find your peace again…Amen.'

Mollie nodded and agreed. That all made perfect sense to her; unlike some prayers, she had been forced to recite.

In a rush of energy, Chloe was out of the car and striding down the street; a woman on a real mission, Mollie nearly running to keep up. Eventually, both a bit breathless, they stood before a Georgian terrace house with imposing steps and iron railings. The doorbell rang in the depths of the house. Chloe rubbed her hands together nervously and reached up to ring again. From inside they heard footsteps on floorboards. A plump man in cords and a checked shirt opened the door.

'Hi, I'm looking for James Whitaker, is he in?' Chloe took mini steps towards the man who turned away.

'James. Visitors. Get yourself down here! Do come in. I expect he'll be a couple of minutes.' He smiled and led them to a beautifully furnished room with a large portrait over the mantlepiece. Mollie and Chloe looked at each other. This wasn't what they had expected. The impression Chloe had got from the report was some kind of squat drug den.

Heavy feet came pounding down the stairs and in came James. In surprise, both women stood up. He was as thin as usual, but with a ruddier complexion, neatly dressed and clean shaven. He took a step back when he saw them.

'Oh, er, Chloe, I guess I owe you an explanation.' He thumped down on the sofa, long limbs sprawling. 'While I was in that hell hole, I did a lot of sorting things out in my head. About you and me and what I want.'

Chloe put a hand on Mollie's arm as she rose to leave.

'It was great meeting you. We had some fun together, but it's not going to work long term for me. I need my freedom. I must do what I want, when I want.' He swung a long leg over the other as he got into his stride. 'A writer needs to be able to experience all things in life to reflect them in his books. And of course, I have my films that I will be involved in when they go into production. I will be flying all around the world; different locations and so on. I need to be free to come and go without ties. I also think that our world visions don't really match. If I need a little recreational drink or other things, that is my responsibility, no one else.'

'So, you're using again already.' Chloe burst in angrily.

He turned to face her. 'Actually no. I'm not, for your information. I picked up the bill myself on the last place, so I don't owe you anything. I'm looking into meditation and herbal teas as a way of helping my writing muse.'

'Anything except for true faith. A real answer that would give you genuine peace?'

'Well, that's arguable…Simon here has been with this guru guy in India. It's amazing what he does.'

'Cop out James, and you know it. All this because I once, and only once asked you if you would like to come to my home group with me. Why is some greasy Indian more appealing? Or is it because I refused to sleep with you? You were rude to my friends who came to dinner that evening.'

'I don't need to be friends with any happy-clappies, thank you.'

'They weren't. If you hadn't stormed out, you would have found one is a publisher, and the other is a recovered addict - unlike you.'

That made James actually look at her and for a moment, they held eye contact. It was like the first time they met; something deeper than all the arguments and differences between them. Chloe broke away this time. Her deeply buried anger at his arrogance and dismissal of everything that was important to her boiled over.

'Enough, James, I've seen and heard all I need from you. Our relationship took you out of your comfort zone, as you needed to make a commitment. For once in your life you had to reach out and give. You could have received real love in return. That was too much for your shallow, selfish, me centred, pig-headed ideology.

You're running scared. It's clear you don't need your support groups anymore. I agree, we are over. I don't want to see or hear from you ever again. Go on in your narrow-minded trough. In the end, you will end up very alone and in a hard place. You'll find that some of the things you mocked me for are true in life and eternity.'

She took a breath. 'Why can you accept all this ridiculous rubbish, that's all lies, and in the same breath dismiss what I believe in. A simple truth that's had over 2000 years of proof. It's as every bit hippie and mystical as all the lies you are accepting now. You won't even try to look beyond religion to the truth. That you can't understand this proves just how completely stupid you are!'

Mollie saw a sneer forming on James' face, but Chloe was on her feet and leaving the room. She followed in the furious wake and cast a glance at James. He was studiously looking at the picture over the fireplace. Chloe slammed the front door behind her, setting the windows rattling. Chloe ran back to the car; forgetting Mollie, who had to bang on the window to get her to open the door.

They sat in silence, Mollie wondering if she had some tissues.

'I feel as if a weight has lifted from me. I said all I had to say. Now I am light and relieved. All this time, thinking is James Ok, where is he? Wondering when he would ring or return my calls. All that pain. I can go back to Wales and get on with my life as it was in its simplicity and kindness.'

Mollie wondered if this wasn't backlash. Chloe turned to her, and she saw that the light was back on in her deep blue eyes.

'Thank you, Jesus!' shouted Chloe, and they took off with a screech of tyres. Mollie was treated to one of the best lunches she had eaten in a long time by the Chloe she had always known.

Chris's day wasn't going so well. As he walked the dogs over to the Manor, Mutantmutt disappeared after a hare. She hadn't come back, despite his bellowing and whistling. When he arrived at the Manor, he found that he had just missed Chloe.

Only Joanna was at home with a squalling baby. 'Oh, don't look so down Chris! I've got something for you. Ignore Amber, she's annoyed because I stopped her emptying the rubbish bin. You would have thought this child had no toys!'

She led the way through the house and Chris slumped on the sofa in the kitchen. Ratty trotted off with Joanna's dogs. All went quiet as Amber gummily inspected Chris from her position on the floor. Joanna disappeared for a moment to the office and then re-appeared with a large bound file, which she handed to him.

'Did you have a good time in Swanage?' Chris hoped Mollie hadn't told Joanna all the details. 'Yes, and I'm returning in a couple of days while those kids are here. I'll return afterwards for a few weeks until I start my new job! I'm going to work in a Fish and Chip shop for the summer.'

'Good grief, you're certainly changing your profession. Since when have you liked cooking?' Much the same reaction as when he had told Mollie. 'It's for the season and I'm glad to be free of milking. Now, what was it you said you had for me?'

'When we heard the tale of your great, great grandfather helping to rescue all the treasures when the original house burnt down, it caught our interest. Especially the bit about how he got the land as a thank-you. As we told you ages ago, we found out a little about your dodgy past, Black Christopher the Highwayman, and all that. We planned to research it, then madam arrived.

However, Jan and Harry had a bit of a lull with the archive business, so they did it for me. We can't find any evidence at all that he might have actually set the fire, only the coincidence that he was given the large plot of land and the farm afterwards. So, we delved right back as far as possible.

The boys have photocopied all the documents they found and have done you a family tree. It's the sort of stuff they do in their sleep! When you have had a read, you don't need to give this back. But we would like to add it to the Hazeley online archive if you're happy with that. You certainly have an interesting family!'

'Thanks so much. I've haven't thought about it at all since you told me, been busy!' He took the heavy book. He sat and talked estate things, including the arrival of Chaos and the Shetland. Amber climbed onto his lap and he couldn't move. Finally, he made his way home. The book was a burden. Mutantmutt was waiting for him at the top of the hill.

He stood for a moment looking down at his farm. It looked so idyllic, the trees coming out, the mares and foals in the blossoming orchard, the cows cudding away. Chaos and Keith grazed, taking a break from their constant games. The grass had that vibrant green. Even the farm, with the old wooden outbuildings and the stone house looked like a picture postcard. He was so lucky to own it, even if right at the moment he didn't particularly want to be there.

In the quiet of the sitting room, with the dogs snoring, he opened the book. It began in the 16th century and followed the line of his family, who were peasants and farmworkers. They had been so all the way to the time when they got the farm from the estate. What caught Chris's attention away from the standard life and death recordings, was the courts, assizes and magistrate's reports. Throughout, there had been criminals and vagabonds in every generation. Cattle and horse thieves, the highwayman, smugglers and wreckers, poachers and tricksters; some even got sent to Australia. All of which stopped when the farm gave them status and an honest living.

He began to peruse the reports. The details of the hanging of the highwayman caught his attention. There was a reference to how they hacked off his long yellow hair beforehand so it wouldn't get in the way of the rope.

So, his hair colour was a genetic thing. Chris unfolded the family tree and spread it out. He searched for Black Christopher, the highwayman and found that he died without children or wife. Possibly that wasn't unexpected. He looked overall and read that in many generations, but not all, there would be one man, with many brothers and sisters who died unmarried and with no recorded descendants.

He checked the names with the court records. They were often the one and the same. The hackles began to rise on the back of his neck, and something started to click into place.

He had always imagined that his condition was a one-off. It now looked like a genetic trace. At least he hadn't taken to violence or theft; but he might have done. A weight descended on him. He was the last in his line; his uncle and aunt were childless. If he had kids, he could pass on this gender mess to another generation.

Searching again, he found the picture of a relation who had died in the First World War. He had blonde hair slicked back. Had he taken a way out or was it the war? What little hope Chris had for a normal family life was now non existent. He was castrated physically and must now be by choice. Even if he did find the courage to go to a hospital to find out what was up, what was the point? His injuries had stopped the little function he had, and he would rather never ride again and live with a little pain than dig any deeper. What hope was there for any relationship? He knew he wasn't gay. He leant towards women, not men, and that made it worse. No one would want him if there could be no family.

Chris hated this farm; what it stood for, a respectability hiding a dark secret. Had his father known? He wanted to lash out, take a horse and gallop it until they were both drenched in sweat, but he couldn't.

Where was Mollie? His compromise friend who would listen and not judge. She cared for him the same, regardless of anything. It was a shame he felt nothing else for her. She would have been a port of refuge. He found no answer and went down the pub. Several hours later, Mollie had to haul him home.

She wouldn't let him get away without a pretty good explanation the next day. With sadness he showed her the book.

'It looks like you're right. It may be a genetic condition; which in this day and age actually might make it simpler. There are all sorts of things that can be done. You've got to face it. Chris, you need to get to a clinic and get some tests done. Consult a surgeon who can sort out your scars.' Trust her to see the practical, matter-of-fact sense side to it all. She couldn't feel the weight he bore; couldn't understand the inner dimension.

'I know, I'm not ready. I'm going to head back today. I've got my laptop and my phone. This time, we will keep in touch.'

'You have moved into the new century at last!' Mollie laughed. 'It's a shame, we haven't had a dog walk together or a trip to the beach. When the lost girls have gone, we can. I hope there will be time before you start work. It is best you shoot off. As much as I hate to say it, I'm certain a couple of the girls will grow into riding club types!' They exchanged the old conspiratorial look.

For a moment Chris was okay, everything was fine. Then the load tried to return. Yet with it came the acknowledgement that if he found a way speak to Mollie about it, he should also talk to Alan. He cursed himself for coming back in the first place. If only Alan and the others hadn't told him that he needed to go home. Without this push, he might simply have found somewhere to rent in Swanage until it was time for his job to start. The restaurant was being decorated. If he hadn't come home, this weight wouldn't have returned.

Even though it had only been a short time, there was a sense of familiarity and even homecoming that filled Chris as he drove down the rutted track to the cottages. No abandoning the truck in the quarry this time. He heard music coming from Alan's cottage. He banged on the door, suddenly a little nervous. Alan's face registered complete surprise.

'Chris, what on earth brings you back so soon? Come in, join us for supper!' He held open the door. The cottage seemed filled with people. Chris took in Eustace, Sam and two others. One was a middle-aged woman with cropped hair, who must be sister Jo. To his surprise, the other was Steve. His visit had paid off after all. One of Sam's cottage pies steamed on the table and they all tucked in; but Chris had a strange sense of dislocation.

He wasn't one of the insiders anymore.

Some of the situations and people they were talking about were unfamiliar to him and he felt left out. In such a short time, too. The stables weren't even mentioned except in passing. He was glad when the plates were cleared. With that, he realised Rex and his love weren't around.

'Where are the dogs?'

'Next door, I'm afraid. Turns out that someone is allergic to dogs!' Alan mock glared at Steve.

'Ok, Ok, Ok, I really will go and get the antihistamines!'

'How're things back at your place? Is Mollie coping?'

Chris smiled. 'Perfectly, as I'm sure Ruth has told you!'

'What brings you back?'

'I was given a present. Joanna's team has done research into my family history. It's turned out that my condition isn't a one-off. It's been carried down through the generations. I am certain now that I can't have kids. Even if it's possible, this mutant gene might be passed on to someone else.'

'But you always thought that. Is it so important?' Alan asked, almost as if he had lost interest in the conversation.

'I wanted to discuss it with someone. Mollie has the lost girls until after Easter, and I didn't want to hang around. She'll have her hands full.'

'Well, let's pray for you, it's getting a bit late. Where are you staying?' asked Eustace.

That hit Chris like a blow. He had been unconsciously relying on staying here. Obviously, the cottages were all full. He reacted rapidly. 'I've got a B&B in Wareham. I'm lucky to have it, being Easter.'

They prayed for him in a general manner. It gave him the sense that they were a gang that didn't want outsiders. He made his leave soon after. Alan came to the door with him as the others cleared up. Outside, they breathed in the air.

'You do need to move on Chris. If you won't go to a clinic and get sorted; you won't be able to find peace. You must pray about it and get to terms with it. Living in this limbo will paralyse you.'

The dogs heard their voices and barked. Alan opened the door, and they received a vociferous greeting. Rex looked well, and while pleased to see Chris, he wasn't all over him.

Still stung by what he took as a rejection, Chris asked, 'Are you and Steve together?'

The brief glimpse on Alan's face told it all. He was in love, even if Steve wasn't.

'Sort of. He found me by chance and has been staying here ever since. We're catching up on things; getting his head around me being me. He's been an Anglican for years; now he is finding out about the wider community of Christ.'

Chris had enough of the dreamy look. Steve might at least have given him and Sue the credit for putting them together. He made his leave; fighting the sense of rejection. The blackness crept over him. In the truck, he rang Sue, but it went through to answerphone. The course was highly intensive with evening study. She didn't have time to talk to him, either.

What should he do? He couldn't face the lost girls. Perhaps he should do what he'd said and drive to Wareham and find a B&B. On the way, he had another idea and swung back to Swanage. It was possible that Mrs Young had a room or would know of one. It could buy him some space to make a plan.

She had her grumpy face on when she opened the door but honoured him with a rare smile when she saw it was him.

'She's not here!' she laughed and let him in.

'I wondered if you know of anyone with a spare room. I need somewhere to stay until my job starts.'

'Sofa's free for tonight. I'll ring round in the morning.' Abrupt as usual, but she softened. 'I'll put the kettle on and then you can tell me what you and Sue have been up to.'

Chris found it difficult on the lumpy sofa. Everything spun around in his head again. The darkness hanging on the edges as ever. Finally, he prayed. Not the wordy stuff that he had been given earlier. His familiar emergency, 'help'. Followed by thanks, as he was filled with peace and what he must do. He slept.

A few days later found Chris in London, standing before the doors of a posh house in Harley street…

Mollie waited in the sunshine for the school minibus to arrive. The return of the girls was a welcome relief after the events of the past few days. A return to horses and simple teenage moodiness, that seemed far less complicated. The girls disgorged with far more cheerfulness than the first time. The whoops and greetings were for Mollie, not just the dogs!

'Only a couple of days and it's chocolate time!' Debbie laughed. This received a stern look from the new nun who had driven them. She nodded cursorily at Mollie, handed a letter, and drove away. The girls were already on their way in.

'Oh, and by the way, we're expecting a roast on Sunday, no more vegan!!!' said Sarah.

'I'm so relieved. Will turkey do?' They cheered and disappeared upstairs. In the kitchen, Mollie revelled in the thumps and bumps above. She opened the letter, which was thankfully a list of term dates and asking her to contact the school about the summer holidays. The nun's glare had made her expect something awful. Mollie's phone rang.

'Hi, it's Mac, we've got a problem. One of the

mares' owners has asked for a fertility test before sending her to Keith. They aren't convinced he's okay after the accident. They don't want to send their mare to have her come back not in foal. We have to do one.' Mollie's heart sank. She knew well what it would entail.

'But we don't have any mares in season or anything else that might do.'

'It's okay. Ann has a mare that's always rampant. If we could get him down there this afternoon, I can send the sample. Otherwise, it has to be after the bank holiday and the sample won't keep.'

'We'll have to box him. I'm not leading or riding him there.'

'But you'll do it?'

Mollie laughed. 'Do I have any choice? I don't want Diane breathing down my neck! What time are we expected?'

'Not till mid-afternoon.'

'Now I have to do a sex education lesson for the girls!' Mac sniggered and rang off.

Soon they all sat around the table with what was hopefully the penultimate vegan meal.

'So, what are all your plans?' Mollie asked.

'Well,' said Debbie, ever the leader. 'We've been doing loads of time in the gym. Miss Masterton has been making us improve our flexibility and strength. We have, obviously a gym horse, but that's not the same. We want to work on the basic levels and moves and go from there.

There's a vaulting club near Stockbridge, which has an event during the holidays. Can we go?'

'Of course. What about actual riding?'

'Well, shall we see how it works out? Ann has booked us all in for sessions after the holiday. We know when and what…but it won't be all of us.' Debbie glared at Sarah, who looked uncomfortable.

'Someone had a big argument with Father Parry and has been in detention. Now she says she doesn't want to vault.'

'That had nothing to do with it!' Sarah was angry. 'We had a long discussion on sin and forgiveness. I'm a year below you. We don't really mix, and I'm okay with that. I want some time out. I want to chill, possibly go hacking. What's wrong with that?'

'Not a problem. I guess we can do a team of three in most of the movements,' said Clare. 'But you haven't told Mollie everything.'

Sarah sighed. 'It was so upsetting when Sister Jo left. She was my mentor, and she didn't even say goodbye. I might just have shouted at Mother Superior a bit…'

Mollie burst out laughing. 'That took courage! Don't worry, Sarah, my goal for all of your time here is that you have a home from home. If you want to veg out for the next two weeks, that's fine with me. Now, if you've finished, we can go and see the foals and my new horse. Afterwards, I'll tell you what I have to do this afternoon.'

They admired the foals, cooing over their cuteness, then they trooped over to the paddock.

'This is Chaos. He's a rescue from some gypsies. I will be breaking him in soon. Don't laugh at him, he doesn't know he looks like a horse colour explosion!' The girls were too interested to laugh and plied her with questions.

'He's amazing, Mollie. How old is he?' Mollie loved their interest. They watched the two horses playing together.

'Now, this afternoon, I have to take Keith down to the yard. He's having a fertility test which means he has to give a sample of semen.' There was a consistent yuck response.

'I'm going to box him there. You can all come too if you want, but I'm not answering any more than basic sex education questions!'

'I think I'll miss that one,' said Sarah. The others wanted to chat with Ann and went to help get Keith in and gave him a groom. Mollie got the travelling gear to wrap him up in. He loaded without a problem, and she heaved an inner sigh of relief.

Mac was already at the yard and the mare in a stable. Keith changed character as he came out of the box. Perhaps he remembered his time there and his bad behaviour, or he smelt the mare. He looked like himself before the accident, full of testosterone.

Opening his mouth, he yelled his loudest whinny; his entire body shaking. Mollie and

Mac got the travelling bandages off as he pivoted around, Ann hanging onto his head. The threesome careered around the back of the yard to the mare's box.

'You're going to have to be flipping quick,' gasped Ann as she hung on. One of the grooms brought the mare out and the horses exchanged snorts. She licked and chewed. She swivelled around and Keith mounted her. Mac got in the way and collected the sample. Keith lay in a heap on the mare's back.

After a moment, he perked up and slid off, obviously tired. Suddenly, his ears pricked, and he whinnied again. There was a commotion around the other side of the block, and they heard shrieks. As if he was trotting back home came Chaos, nickering for his mate.

'What the dickens! Someone fetch a halter!' shouted Ann. Debbie appeared with one, the girls having kept out of the way. Chaos was calm, and this quietened Keith too, all interest in the mare lost.

'How on earth did he get here and so quickly?' Mollie looked around.

'He must have jumped out of the field. He was up the far end grazing when we drove out,' said Jenny in astonishment. 'That's a big fence.'

'And we have to keep him in it,' groaned Mollie. Now she had to sort out separation anxiety as well as break in her horse. 'Let's take these two back.'

The girls were all in slightly embarrassed mode, but they helped load up. Chaos, now with his buddy, was quite happy. The girls accredited him with great hearing and navigational skills for finding Keith from only a whinny. Mollie cooked, and they watched a film, but the girls were tired and made an early night, which she thought must be a first.

Sarah had been quieter than usual and later on came down to the sitting room where Mollie lay chilling on the sofa. She remembered their first night and felt pleased that this time was different. Sarah held a letter in her hand.

'What was Sister Jo doing here?' Mollie turned surprise. 'How did you find out that?' She had to admit it. 'She was here for a while before she moved on to her new home.'

'It was horrible when she just suddenly left. No one would tell me where she had gone. It was as if suddenly she never existed...' Sarah looked as if she might cry.

'She told me that they considered it would be less disruptive that way. She couldn't do anything about it. Where did you find the letter?'

'Inside one of the books I left behind. She doesn't say much, only wishes me well and to be friendly with her replacement. But Sister Isabella is such a pain. She's so conventional. Why does a nun stop being a nun?'

'I have no idea. One never left when in my schooldays. I guess it's something you sign up for your whole life. You don't expect to leave.' Mollie panicked inside. How much could and should she say?

'I so missed our chats. She was so open to all I asked. I would like to see her again, but she didn't leave an address. Of course, you know where she is?'

'Yes, but we can't pop round there; it's too far away. She is starting a new life and may not want to look back; however hard that is.'

'Would you contact her and ask her, anyway? I need to catch up with her and say a proper goodbye.'

That sounded quite adult and reasonable. 'I'll drop her a line and we'll go from there. That's the best I can do.'

Sarah smiled and left. Mollie was glad that Ruth had at least tried to say goodbye.

Next morning, Mollie woke early, alerted by the girls acting like kids and shouting about chocolate. So much for not eating before Mass. Or were things different now? They all bundled into the Land Rover and Mollie, having declined the invitation to join them, took the dogs for a walk.

As she walked in the fields, she heard the bells being rung at communion. It all seemed such a waste of time; all that empty ritual and smoke making. She couldn't remember how she had formed all her opinions. Apart from Sarah, the girls accepted it all and appeared content; even surprised when questioned on it. Blind faith? Why had she rejected it? Did it relate to the time God had failed her when she asked him to make her parents love her? Had that been a wrong question? Was he trying to tell her something?

The school apparently had two sorts of girls. Ones like herself who were injured and abandoned and those who were getting on with life, unquestioning and seemingly content. There seemed to be no middle line; you were in or out. Not that she hadn't tested the boundaries. She suddenly brought to mind being sent to Chapel with Father Howard, where he took her to task for all the things she said about God. He made her pray for forgiveness rather than give her some sort of answer to her dilemmas. He wouldn't even listen to her and instead had given her the hell and damnation stuff.

There must be another side. Chloe and Joanna had such a simple, happy relationship in their faith. Even Chris hung onto what he believed despite all the unhappiness; it kept him going.

Yes, there had to be more to all this, but did she really want to go deeper? She was quite happy as she was, wasn't she? Something rose in her. An anger and a fear. All right, God, if you're so real and true, prove it to me. Make it so clear that I will understand it. There'll be no doubt it is you, and I'll be convicted that you do exist. Then I might think about you a bit more. But I'm not doing the church rules, smoke and confession stuff.

Grimly determined, she strode on fiercely,

leaving behind the dogs who were paddling in the river. The church bells rang, and she realised she needed to hurry on. The girls stood outside the church looking slightly gobsmacked.

'I can see the nuns turning and running away from him!' laughed Debbie. 'No books, no smoke. He didn't even have a dog collar on.'

Sarah butted in. 'We had songs on a projector. Totally funky and loud, but so true for Easter...that one about Mary meeting Jesus in the garden and calling him master.'

'That was completely cool. I've never been to a service like it. We all got an egg!' Clare said through chocolate.

'So, you all enjoyed yourselves? Is that so unusual?'

'YES!' came the unanimous chorus.

They drove home; the girls trying to remember the tunes, looking them up on their phones and learning the words. Mollie felt overwhelmed by their happiness; it was almost tangible. Easter lunch consisted of turkey with all the trimmings. Afterwards they insisted on watching several chick films. Monday, they all rode out with Ann and Mollie. Mollie was filled with a pure joy to be with them; such fun. Had her teenage been so?

Mollie, still full of food and chocolate, rolled over with a groan when the phone rang early on Tuesday morning.

'Hi, it's Mac. Euston, we have a problem.' If

he was joking, there must be a real problem. Mollie sat up blearily, sending the dogs to the floor. 'Our dear fellow Keith is completely and utterly sterile.' He paused to let Mollie gather her wits.

'You jest?'

'Oh, no. It must have been the trauma from the accident. He has so few sperm and they all need water wings. They are so deformed.' Mollie thought of the effects.

'Have you told Diane?'

'Ummm, not to her face. They're in somewhere without signal, so I've sent emails and texts. At least she might have time to calm down before I speak to her.'

'I suppose I have to cancel all the bookings. Oh no, Chris has taken his laptop with him, I don't think I've copied them… give me a bit of time and I'll call you back?' Her first reaction was to ring, email and text Chris. There was no reply. It might be she had a copy on her computer.

She rushed down and powered it up to find it was already on and in sleep mode. Hadn't she shut it down last time? The search was to no avail, and she cursed herself for not copying the files. She had relied on Chris's return before the mares started arriving in the next few weeks. She was looking through all the emails when Debbie put her head around the door.

'Um, has Sarah gone for a walk or is doing something with the cows?'

'Why?'

'Because we can't find her.'

'WHAT??!!' Mollie leapt up and ran up the stairs. The bed was made, and no bright pink backpack on the back of the door. Mollie bit back a rude word. What was she going to do? She envisioned fraught parents, the police, having to face up to Mother Superior, the newspapers… it ran on.

'Where could she have gone?' Mollie muttered in desperation. She looked at the computer again as if it would bring an answer. 'Hang on a minute Debbie, I have an idea.'

Mollie scrolled through the last opened documents, and she realised. Sneaky, poor girl. Sarah had been through the emails and opened up one from Ruth. With no password on the system she had walked right in. How did she know that Ruth was her real name? Some sleuthing and determination there. Mollie read the email and found the address of the cottages Ruth had sent it in case any mail needed forwarding on.

'I know where she's gone. Give me a couple of minutes to ring Ruth and warn her. We'll have to go and pick Sarah up, she can't have got there yet… I hope.'

Again, Mollie was frustrated as Ruth didn't pick up on either the landline or the mobile. She began to seethe with impatience.

'Hey, keep cool Moll!' said Debbie.

'You've found her. Come and have a coffee. We can all talk it over. The others are getting up.'

Taking this most sensible course, Mollie took a deep breath and tried to slow her pounding heart. The girls in various stages of PJs joined them and made breakfast around Mollie, who was still reeling.

'So, where is she?' demanded Jenny. 'She seemed fine yesterday. I don't get why she would need to bolt.'

Mollie came clean. 'Well, it's Sister Jo. She had formed some sort of attachment to her.'

'What, that old trout!' said Debbie, then straightened her face.

'Look, I don't know what kind of home life you lot have. But Sarah strikes me as someone who doesn't get a lot from her parents. Ruth, er, I mean Sister Jo, somehow filled that gap. Sarah was upset that she wasn't allowed to say goodbye. Perhaps she just wants some closure. That's not unreasonable.'

'Yeah, she did seem to vanish into thin air.' Jenny handed Mollie a mug of coffee. 'So, we go and haul her back?'

'I'm tempted not to rush and let them share some time together,' Mollie sighed. 'But I'm responsible for her. Can one of you look at the bus and train times to Swanage, and then on to Worth Matravers?' She sipped her coffee as they searched.

'And there's bad news. You remember that Keith's test?' They unanimously cringed. 'Well, the poor old boy is infertile. Completely firing blanks. I can't get in contact with Chris, who has all the bookings for the season on his PC, and I may have to deal with his owner, and she can be well… um… interesting.'

'What will happen to him?' asked Clare.

'I've no idea. He has no value as a stud anymore, and he's too volatile to be a riding school horse. He's about 10 already.'

'You don't think?' asked Jenny, looking pale. Mollie understood the unasked question.

'It's a possibility.' Mollie tried to smile.

'If she left on the 6 am bus, she will reach Matravers by about two this afternoon,' Debbie changed the subject. 'How long does it take in the car?'

'A couple of hours at the most, depending on traffic.'

Mollie's phone rang. It was an international number. 'Oh, hi Diane. Yes, Mac has told me. You what? No, I'm just chasing Chris to get the bookings to cancel them.' She used her best pony soothing voice.

The girls listened in. 'You what? Yes, I can contact the insurance company. You want what?' It was Mollie's turn to go pale. 'Yes, I understand he has no value anymore. Don't you think we shouldn't rush into snap decisions? That's a good idea if you're on your way back. I'll keep you informed…' Mollie hung up with a sense of both relief and dread.

'You got all that?'

They nodded, for once lost for words. 'It

seems so unfair. He hasn't done anything wrong,' wailed Jenny. Mollie put her arm around her. 'We have to go and get Sarah. Now, you can all go to the stables as planned or you can come with me'. The girls looked at each other.

'We'll go down to the horses if that's okay...it's not our problem.' So much for sticking together, thought Mollie as they collected their gear and left the house. She had a quick word with Ann who agreed to keep them on as long as possible, and then roared away into the morning traffic.

It was a pleasant drive after all, and Mollie wondered if she might actually arrive before Sarah; that would change a lot of things. She drove through Wareham and switched the Tom Tom on to find her way through the quiet lanes. Just after Corfe Castle, she turned right and up a steep hill, narrowly missing a bus.

Then more lanes. She came to a large house, and followed orders to go down a rutted lane, past some stables. Then she slammed the brakes on. In front of her shone the deepest blue sea and a row of stone cottages by a stream running to the beach. She opened the door and leapt out. The dogs streaked past her with huge glee. From nowhere came Rex and a red spaniel; there was much leaping and barking. Then in general good will they took off as a pack to the sea.

'They look as though they've met before and it's time to catch up!'

Mollie jumped out of her skin to find a short dark-haired man, with a big smile on his face behind her.

'Hi, I'm Alan!' and he stretched his hand out to shake. Mollie looked closely at the mysterious Reverend. He looked quite normal and not at all feminine. 'You must be Mollie! The hair gives it away.' He laughed into her eyes; he was already a friend.

'Chris told me a lot about you too!' Mollie smiled back.

'We don't need to go through all that then! How's Chris doing?'

'I can't find him, and I must speak to him urgently. We have a problem with one of the horses.'

'Keith?'

'Who else!'

Alan grinned again and changed the subject.

'Madam arrived late last night in a taxi. She slept on Ruth's sofa and we were wondering what to do with her!'

He led the way to the end cottage and knocked on the door. 'All respectable ladies?'

Ruth opened up with a big grin on her face. 'We wondered how long it would take you to find her. She wouldn't let me ring you.' Sarah peered sheepishly around her.

'Sorry, Mollie…I've been told to say that!'

'You all seem very happy considering what she's done! Just as well, I hadn't contacted her parents. Why couldn't you just wait a couple of days?' Mollie was cross now.

'I just needed to say goodbye. It's all been hanging over me. I wanted to understand why she didn't want to be a nun and what she was doing. Everything's sorted now.' she grinned again with the simplicity of childhood. Mollie saw they were all looking at her, so she gave in.

'What can I do? No harm's done!' She fed on the good humour.

'Good, glad that's sorted. Come and have some lunch!' Ruth held open the door, and they all trooped in. Just at that moment, four very wet dogs rushed in to join the meal.

'Who invited you?' Ruth stood and looked at them. To Mollie's astonishment, the dogs sat down and wagged their tails at her.

'Now, if you're good, you'll get snacks after. Go and lie down.' Mollie felt her jaw drop as all the dogs as one ran and piled into a huge dog sofa at the back of the room. With a collective sigh, they lay down. Their eyes watched Ruth's every move.

'She has a gift with animals, doesn't she?' exclaimed Sarah.

'I agree. I've seen her effect on the horses,' Mollie laughed. 'She could make a career with it!'

Ruth jumped and looked at her. 'People keep on saying that to me! And I'm beginning to think they might have a case!'

They all sat down, and Mollie found a table set for all four of them. 'You expected me this quickly?'

'We just knew,' smiled Ruth.

The whole matter of Sarah's bolt seemed to be forgotten, and the meal was spent in catching up on news. Clearly, Ruth had put her demons behind her, put on weight, and was tanned. She smiled and smiled. It was extraordinary. The plates were cleared, and the dogs came eagerly for their treats. Then they all poured out into the sunshine. Mollie sat with them on a bench while Sarah ran to the waves with the dogs.

'Is she okay?'

'Yes, she just likes things in boxes and closure. It makes her safe. She simply needed to say her farewells; to be sure that I hadn't lost my faith. She even brought a whole document she wrote to convince me that Jesus does love me even if I'm not a nun or even a Catholic anymore!' They laughed.

'How are you? Is it all well with you?' Mollie knew Ruth wasn't asking about work.

'Yes. It was most strange, when I was out with the dogs yesterday, I made a deal with God. If he proves he exists; I agreed that I might chat to him a bit more!' Mollie blushed.

'Well, keep me informed. I'll be interested to hear what he gets up to!' Ruth burst out laughing. Mollie was astonished. She had expected a lecture on gravity with God, but that was Jo. She liked this new Ruth. This little enclave appeared to have a good effect on people.

'Please tell me when Chris returns,' Alan

suddenly broke in. 'I've been taken to task rather a lot about when he visited. He brought this book which showed that there had been a long line of people in his family with our problem. Steve had just arrived, and I was a bit caught up with it all. I gave him short shrift and then he disappeared.'

Soon Mollie found herself propelled back to the Land Rover with two sorry dogs who clearly wanted to stay. They drove away with Sarah hanging out the window, waving farewells.

'Look, there are the stables that Chris worked in. I wish there had been time to visit the horses, but I guess we might visit Ruth again? She was so kind when I turned up, and she explained it all well to me. Ruth is just following what she must do, and it's Jesus who's taking her to the new phase of her life. It all seems so right. Perhaps nuns should sign up for a fixed contract where they can leave or stay on as Daddy does with the army!'

Mollie snorted, 'Couldn't you see Mother superior bullying people to stay?'

'Yes, completely, possibly it's better that way, but I will have something to say to her on how it upset me. Ruth says she will come here before we go back to school too.'

'Have you thought about what the others might think of that?'

'Do them good. Show them there is life after nuns.'

Sarah, the budding radical, talked and talked like a burst dam all the way back. Mollie let it flow over her. It was a wave of joy. This was the old Sarah, not the sad creature of the past couple of days.

When they drove into the yard, they found other girls in the arena in their vaulting gear. They were all grouped around Barney, who was having his front leg examined by Ann. Something was very wrong.

'It's no good. I think he has pulled a tendon, but there's more to it than that. This constant work on the left rein has put his back out. Combined with the unusual pressure on his spine from you standing and the pair work. I have other groups who use him too. Basically, he's too old, and it's too late for him to adjust his muscles for this new regime. I'm sorry girls, but we have to find another horse, a younger one who we can train to the discipline.'

The girls all looked sad. They then saw Mollie and Sarah.

'Looks like we're stuffed for any competitions this summer,' moaned Jenny.

'No, don't be so down,' interjected Ann. 'I have lots of contacts and it shouldn't be too difficult to find a horse. You lot are going to that open night next week, so you might make new friends then. It's not the end of the world! Hi Sarah, all okay now?'

The girls looked with little interest; they weren't bothered about Sarah. She appeared to read this, and to Mollie, shrivelled like a deflated balloon. Mollie had to do something to rescue the situation.

'How about we drop these wet dogs back home and then go and get a Pizza? Everything's back to normal after the holiday!' That seemed to meet a point, and they all piled into the Land Rover, making disgusted comments on stinking dogs.

The next few days went well, or so Mollie thought, no more dramas. The girls did some practice on the wooden horse, rode, shopped. Sarah's little trip appeared to be forgotten. It hadn't registered on their scales. Sarah spent time with Mollie, chatting away, and even once got Mollie into a conversation about God.

Then finally came the day of the vaulting demonstration. They all packed eagerly into the Land Rover and chugged up the motorway. The event was smaller than Mollie had imagined, but it didn't stop the girl's excitement; even Sarah was keen.

A couple of horses were being warmed up. Around them all sizes of girls in wonderfully coloured costumes were doing stretches and warming up too.

The indoor school had a small arena laid out with white bricks, with seats so they all piled in and got a front row. But there weren't many people there. Then loud music came on, and in came a team of five. The girls wore purple leotards, hair tight in buns and heavy makeup. Mollie heard some muttering in the background about palette knife make up, and she tried not to snigger.

A huge, wide black cob followed the team. He looked completely bored with the whole thing. The lunger took him into the middle and got him going on a steady circle. At her prompt, the team trotted in and formed a row at the edge. They then jogged in and the acrobatics began. Just as the first girl got on board, there was a loud crackle from a loudspeaker system. The horse jumped, and she nearly fell off, but she cleverly righted herself.

The booming voice then proceeded to describe each movement in turn with so many technical names and details that after a while Mollie switched off and watched the show. It almost took her back to the old circuses, with the women jumping on and off. It must be the roots of all this.

It was fascinating, but Mollie couldn't help thinking it was more about the gear and gymnastics than horsemanship. The girls finished with all 5 in various positions on the horse and the small audience, who Mollie guessed were mostly families, clapped and cheered. Then came an invitation to go in and meet the team and the horse. So of course, the girls rushed in there, and Mollie found herself with Sarah.

'It's not for me, all that paint, and I'm not that energetic!' she said. They watched as Debbie who had been chatting with the oldest girl was legged up onto the horse. He leapt straight into a canter, and Debbie with great care got herself up onto her knees and spread her arms, a huge grin on her face. She held it for a while, then sat again, then dismounted over the hindquarters.

'I understand you've brought the girls over?' Mollie jumped at the loud voice. A tall, well-muscled woman in heavy makeup grinned down at her; it was the microphone voice.

'Yes, they're just staying with me over the holidays.'

'Wonderful, we're always looking for new members for the club. Maybe you can bring them in term time too? We meet on Saturday evenings and sometimes during the week if we're preparing for a competition.' She obviously hadn't registered a word Mollie said.

'Your girls say they have lost their horse, as it's lame.' She sighed. 'It's such a problem finding a good one that can take the work. My name's Laura and you are?'

'Mollie. But as I said, the girls are boarders at St Anne's, so they will have to arrange it with the school in term time, but we can certainly come during the holidays if they want to!' She smiled, getting the idea that this woman was of the old school type PE teacher who would bulldoze everything.

'Super, now I must go and chat with the mums.' She was off, and Sarah heaved a sigh of relief. 'Definitely not for me, I'd rather stay with Ann!'

The girls were so excited and dragged Mollie over to meet the team, all talking at once, making plans, telling her all the moves, exchanging phone numbers. Suddenly, Mollie had total peace in the middle of this tumult. She had done what she wanted to do; given some lost girls a sense of identity. They had something to do; a secure home for their holidays, with her as their base. A home from home. Even Sarah trusted her with her deeper turmoil; even if she was a Sister Jo substitute. She felt highly protective and loving to them all. She had succeeded.

The rest of the holidays were pure joy to Mollie. The girls rode and shopped, if possible, even more. Sarah tried even more to evangelise Mollie, but she resisted every argument; sometimes playing the devil's advocate when she secretly agreed.

They joined the club and made plans to go during the summer holidays if they came to the farm. Some like Debbie, thought they might be with their parents somewhere hot and sunny, so it was all a bit up in the air. Sarah was fairly certain she would be there, but as Mollie explained, the door remained open; they just needed to tell her if and when. There were no more calls from Diane, and the subject of Keith was sort of swept under the table. Most of all, Mollie hoped that Chris would finally return as he said he promised, so at least they could cancel the bookings.

In the aftermath of the girls, Mollie had

things to catch up on. Post and bills to be paid before she could go and play with her pony. She also needed to ring the electrician as the internet kept on going down. With a mug of coffee, she worked her way through her tasks. The last letter was handwritten in a vaguely familiar scrawl. As she took in the words, she was torn between anger and astonishment.

Mollie.

I've got one of the people leaving to post this for me, as I'm not supposed to communicate as I go through this ridiculous drying out process. You will be hearing from the clinic in due course as they ask relatives to visit at some stage, and I want to pre-empt them doing the dirty on me.

I understand that I came to see you; to let you know about your father, but I cannot remember it. But I have known for a long time that I owe you a deeper explanation of things. I wasn't born wealthy, just a council house in Basingstoke. Dad was unemployed and drank. He beat Mum and abused me. She wouldn't let me call the police, or even run to somewhere safe. It made me decide that I wasn't going be in such a position, let alone have children. Women are weak. If I could have changed into a man, I would have done so. As soon as I could I left home. I made sure I wasn't going to be in that situation in my life. I worked and studied, and then started the business when I saw a gap. I was correct and the business thrived.

Then I was threatened with a takeover, so I used my wits to seduce the son of the director. Only trouble being that he insisted on marriage. With my business at stake, I gave in. I made sure we made a good pre-nuptial and then he did the dirty on me and returned to his playboy lifestyle. But that suited me fine, I had my business and plenty of assets. Then the father-in-law started throwing his weight about, wanted a grandson and heir. I could sympathise with his point. Again, I gave in, on the condition it was done with IVF, so there was no chance it would be a girl. You can guess the rest. We sued the clinic out of existence. The old boy was quite happy at first but soon expected more babies. Then he conveniently died. Your father started going all gooey and talking about more babies too, so I shifted you out of the house to school and got nannies and kept him busy until he forgot about you except in passing.

I've already told you why I never wanted you and you're living up to all my expectations. You'll probably marry some lout, who'll drink any money you have, and you'll never make anything of yourself. I'm glad we signed you out of inheriting. I will sell the business to John and spend the money, or give it to charity, so there will be nothing to inherit, anyway.

But when you come to my meeting, I expect you to behave yourself and not disclose any of this. I have told you it all now, and it will go no further. This is personal and private. I'll not have it discussed in front of the plebs who are here with me.

The letter wasn't even signed. Nothing changes, thought Mollie. But I do have a chance for revenge at the meeting, or not. For once in my life, I have the upper hand over her. That is quite sweet. Surely drying out must have had some positive effect, even though she's just as bad as usual? Can't be much of a therapy they're giving her. Mollie chucked the papers on the heap. Yes, she would have liked her mother to turn a corner and they could be friends, but this obviously was not going to happen. Why did she even write the letter? Was she scared she might go to pieces and reveal all this on the day?

But Mollie wasn't her mother. She would find love; well she had, suddenly thinking of Gary. Maybe they would marry and have loads of children, and they could grow up to be farmers or lawyers. She would be happy, which was something her mother had never experienced. She felt a twinge of sorrow for her but dismissed it, threw the letter down and marched out into the sunshine.

She hadn't been able to do much with Chaos except groom him and Keith while the girls were around, but now she had the whole day to herself. She wondered if he would nap at being taken away from Keith, so she brought him into a box and gave him a huge illicit haynet, which he quickly tucked in to.

Chaos stood happily on the yard. Now that

his winter coat was gone, Mollie stepped back and looked at her wonderfully pink horse. She had never seen anything like him, and those eyes. She had feared that they meant he was wild, but they were kind. His mane was growing at a rate of knots; he could take on a Friesian for the quality. She saw that his tail would soon be on the ground. She knew it was wrong, and that it shouldn't be done alone, but every indication he had given her was that breaking him in wasn't going to be a problem, and he might even be so already.

She looted some tack from Chris's tack room. She took the largest snaffle bit she could find, along with the biggest saddle. Totally naughty, she slipped the halter down his neck and presented him with the bridle. Her instincts had been correct; he lowered his head to the bit and opened his mouth like an expert. She was careful not to bang his teeth and set up any problems. But no, the bridle fitted, even if on the last holes all round. She looped his enormous forelock through and plaited it, so it hung away from his eyes.

She gently placed the saddle on his back. No reaction. It wasn't a perfect fit, but his back was wide and round. With the fleece she had put under, for a short ride it should be comfy.

Mollie put on a body protector and a new hat. There was no turning back. She led him up to the steps by the old dairy; no way she would be able to mount from the ground. Talking to him gently, she stopped him and stepped up. He stood. Didn't budge as she swung her leg over, adjusted her girth and stirrups. No way he wasn't broken in, and it had been well done too.

She took the reins, gave a gentle squeeze, and they marched away. No short cobby step, but that long swinging reach she had guessed about from watching him. His scope reminded her of Challenger, but there the likeness ended. He walked briskly and happily, no sign of panicking for Keith. Maybe it was the being left behind that caused the problem, Molly mused, then suddenly realised she should concentrate.

Where to go? Gary's! She swung Chaos along the grass-covered lane, it was only a couple of miles around the hill, just enough for a first outing. The warm air of the dry spring which made the farmers mutter into their beer about the hay crop had her exhilarated and full of joy. She called to the dogs, who had been asleep in the barn. They followed her, ever eager for an outing.

Throwing caution to the wind, she shortened up and asked him for a trot. He understood the aids and took off. It seemed hugely fast, but it was simply his size, his long legs and being up so high. There was something special about riding a big horse. His breathing was good, so when she was within half a mile from Gary's, she sat deep and asked for canter. Pure, absolute heaven; like the most enormous rocking horse! Fast compared to smaller horses, but almost in slow motion. The dogs were flat out, trying to keep up. Mollie grinned like an idiot, but didn't care as they slowed and swung into Gary's yard.

He was tinkering with a tractor and looked up in surprise as they rollicked across the tarmac. 'You do know that your hair clashes with that beast, don't you?' he grinned. 'Wow, that's a long way up!' He peered up at her. 'And I haven't seen you this happy for ages. I take it he's completely and utterly trained?'

'I have someone to thank for doing an amazing job!' Mollie laughed back. 'When he's settled and I've got a better saddle, you must ride him too; he's just perfect. Then we can find you a horse and do some long-distance trails…'

He saw the faraway look again and was happy for her. The past couple of weeks, despite her protests to the contrary, had seemed to take something away from her. They stood for a second, enjoying the peacefulness. Gary was just going to suggest a coffee, when Chaos suddenly swung around, his ears pricked.

'Oh, no, Gary, the separation anxiety is kicking in, hang on to him.' As he did, they could both hear on the wind a frantic neigh coming from the direction of the farm. Chaos raised his head and bellowed a response.

Gary not being horse wise even though strong, didn't have a firm enough hold. The reins were torn from his hands and, with a half rear, Chaos took off. Mollie kept her seat and, knowing she couldn't stop him, took a handful of mane and leant forward into the speed. It was both terrifying and exhilarating as they belted back down the track.

At least the ground was flat, but a couple of times, Chaos raised his head and bellowed back to his friend, banging Mollie's nose hard as he did. She buried her nose further and tried to predict when he would again; the farm drew closer. Why did she smell smoke in his hair?

Earlier that day, Alan and Ruth squeezed into the mini were bumping up the lane from the cottages towards the main road.

'Are you totally sure that he will be there when we get there?' Ruth wasn't sure.

'When I prayed this morning, I sensed strongly in my spirit that Chris is at the farm and, in some measure, he needs me. I've never had such a conviction before, and I must follow it. I couldn't live with myself if I didn't.' He smiled at her and she perceived the peace on his face.

Ruth wriggled in the tight seat. 'Well, I guess we'll find out soon enough. I so want to chat to Mollie more about animals. Like you, I've also had this conviction, but it's a gentler, growing thing that I have some sort of calling with people and animals. Despite what I've been reading on the internet, I must talk to someone on the business. She's going to laugh so much when she hears I've had riding lessons, let alone wearing jodhpurs!'

'Exchanging one uniform for another! I also need to apologise to Chris for sending him away, So caught up in my feelings for Steve; I was utterly selfish. Chris isn't healed yet, he's so scared of what might happen in a clinic, that he feels it's better to go on maimed and in pain when there could be so much help for him.

He still isn't secure in his identity with Jesus. He just can't see that it doesn't matter what he is; it's his relationship with Jesus that matters... I've failed him when he was with us, we didn't address it properly or pray with him about it.'

Ruth put a steadying hand on his on the wheel. 'You've said so before,' she said gently. 'There's going to be time to tell him, I'm sure. Relax and stop beating yourself up. God has his hand on it. If your feeling is right, today will be his breakthrough.'

Chris and Sue were also making tracks to the farm. Music played in the cab and they ate chips as they drove.

'Are you really sure, really, really sure Chris?'

'Look, as I've said, the mares are no use to me. I'm rethinking entirely what I want to do with the farm. You can use the girls for the RDA work and then you will have the foals to break in and train them as therapy horses. I'd rather you have them than sell them on. There is a sort of relationship to my folks and maybe, just maybe, I can't quite let go yet. The box is big enough for all four, and Mollie can bring them over. It's a win, win for you!'

'Well, if you're sure!'

'SUE!' shouted Chris in exasperation, and then laughed. 'You get me every time! Don't let me forget to give Mollie the file with the Keith bookings. I've no idea why I didn't leave it with her.'

'How long will you be in the clinic?'

'I'm not sure. I only got the date for the first consultation.'

'Were they very annoyed when you turned down the job?'

'No, there are always people looking for work in the season.'

'Then what will you do? I've already offered you the second bedroom in the stable flat.'

'Go back to the farm, I suppose, and think again. Get the hay in. See to the cows. You know, I hate going back there at the moment. As we get closer and closer, my heart is sinking. It's like the weight of my family and ancestors are a pain in my heart.' He was lost in his thoughts, and Sue let him be. He'd been in an odd frame of mind this morning and wouldn't talk about the previous evening.

Chris saw that door at the clinic, and

how he had yet again bottled out on something important in his life. He had walked away and hit the tourist trail, doing Buckingham Palace and all the rounds, anything except think. He saw again the sleazy hotel he stayed in, and the even sleazier clubs that he had visited.

No one attacked him or even found him interesting. He found temporary drinking buddies and people with some coloured pills. Still hurting from Alan's rejection, he had embraced it all, but only to come back to his slutty bedroom. Only himself to face. He had been so confident when he left Mollie; that the effect of the horrible book and his macabre ancestors would be shaken off when he got himself sorted. The peace that had come with his decision to go to the clinic was the right one, but with that first failure, it disappeared.

Each morning, he was back at the door, hangover, trance-like state or not. It took over two weeks of spiralling self-disgust and embittered railing at God before he stepped in and sorted things out.

One morning, Chris stood at his usual dither point, about to turn away, when someone else came up the steps behind him.

'Oh, after you!' This all that was needed, and he found himself impelled through the door to the reception. After all that time dithering, there was a short waiting list, but he did have an initial consultation booked and that was enough. He couldn't give up on that; something concrete to hold on to; he would follow it through.

He looked to find the person who followed him, but there was no one on the waiting room. He or she must have gone in although he hadn't heard and name called.

Chris packed his bags and drove back to Swanage. In this mood of determination, he chucked his job. Not without some regret, but there would be other holiday seasons. He discovered Sue back at Mrs Youngs, getting ready to move up to her flat at the stables. He had helped her with all the boxes and unpacking.

They celebrated her independence with some champagne and then had the most revealing conversation. To his own complete and utter surprise, Chris found himself telling her his life story. It all came pouring out, and he found Sue a good listener. He held back nothing and expected her to chuck him out for being a perv. But she seemed to understand and gave nothing but sympathy, no criticism and back chat; let him flow. She didn't flinch at all the details, nor as he tried with less confidence to explain his faith. When his words had run out, they were quiet for a while.

'Shall I go now?' he finally asked.

'Why, you twit? Don't you realise a lot of this I had guessed; some Alan told me. If not quite the technical details, but mostly that you are in a mess with who you are. I've been mentored by Eustace, I made a commitment a while ago, even if I'm not waving my fish symbols and saying The

Lord every five minutes!' She grinned at him and a little of the weight lifted.

'Let me tell you something about me, and like you, not a lot of people know about the me inside. I grew up in an abusive house. Mum had blokes in and out all the time, and I got fed up with the stream of uncles. Some were nice and life was bearable, and some were sneaky, nasty, low life.

The worst one came last. He came into my room late one night and tried it on. Now, as you can guess, I'm a fighter, and I gave him back. The only trouble he was twice my size. He kicked me so hard in the stomach that I passed out. I woke up to find him raping me. I fought again and he beat me once more before leaving.

Mum was out cold, not hearing a thing. I found I was bleeding from inside. I called an ambulance and crawled out into the street to wait for them. I stayed two months in hospital. He so injured me that they had to give me a hysterectomy besides remove my spleen.

There I was at 15 with the menopause. No egg harvest, so I'm completely infertile. Mum even claimed it was my own fault for leading him on, but social services stepped in and I ended up in various homes. I got rid of my pain in drink and drugs and thieving, so I understand so well where you are.

You could say that we are both sexless, you by birth, me by violence. I sympathise totally with how you are, your self-hatred. But we are both perfect in Jesus. He doesn't care if we're boy, girl, or whatever. He loves us and that's what matters. We may not be able to have all the things in life that others expect, but there are always other directions.

I believe, like any sin, if you were to make a relationship with another man, or me another woman, and call it marriage, he isn't going to like that. It would be a strain on our relationship with him, but he wouldn't stop loving us for being stupid kids. I don't think it is wrong for someone to love someone of the same gender. It's when we confuse that love with sex and make it into a marriage that it's wrong. Look at David and Jonathan. They loved each other but nothing more...' She was running out of verbal steam.

She got up and came over to him, took his face in her hands and kissed him softly on the lips. 'Now you know what I feel about you. All this stuff you're going through means nothing to me. I can sense who and what you are and what you could become. That's what matters.' Chris was dumbfounded, but suddenly, very, very, happy.

So now in the thrall of something new, where neither understood the rules, the boundaries or if it would work, they made their way back to the farm.

Mollie and Chaos hurtled into the yard, to where

Keith hung half out of the stable door, kicking it like fury. Chaos slid to a stop and Mollie would have been over his shoulder if he hadn't such a long neck and so much mane. The two huffed and nickered at each other. She watched for a moment, then Keith was off again; banging at that door and trying to get out. Chaos turned as if to bolt away again.

Then she smelt smoke, and she looked to the farmhouse. The roof was well and truly alight. She could hear crackling and snapping of timbers. What to do? She slithered off Chaos, pulled his tack off, and let it fall to the ground. She reached between the two and opened Keith's door.

To her horror, Chaos pushed inside. It was going to be Black Beauty and the fire all over again. She pinned back the door and ran down to fling wide the field gate.

She pushed into the box of thrashing horses and yelled at the top of her voice, 'GET OUT OF HERE!' plus any other swearwords she could think of. She smacked both on the rumps and this had enough effect to get Keith half out, so she shoved Chaos, followed his buddy.

Heaving at that enormous backside, she pushed enough of him out and reach to shut the door; in her terror, ripping the hook out of the wall. Keith's instinct took over and he bolted to the field; his place of safety and Chaos followed. Gate shut tight, the two horses took off to the highest point where they finally stood and calmed down.

She grabbed her phone and dialled 999. She knew better than to go in the building. Gary arrived in his car with the dogs in the back; the whole horse thing must have only taken moments after all. They stood bewildered as the flames leapt from the main house to the barn. It had the makings of an inferno. Apart from the crackling, all was in a sort of suspended quietness as if the fire sucked the energy out of the air. A red mini pulled into yard. Mollie ran to warn them and found it was Alan and Ruth.

'Don't park here, the whole lots going to go up if the wind goes on blowing in this direction and the fire brigade doesn't come in time.'

'Isn't there a water hose anywhere?' Ruth shouted. That put Gary into action. He ran to the slurry pit and pulled the hose out and started spraying the roof.

Chris's blue truck pulled into the yard. He and Sue piled out. For a second, they looked horrified and froze to the spot.

'Gary!' Chris suddenly shouted. 'Don't put it out, let it burn!' They all turned to him shocked.

'But your insurance won't pay!'

'Don't care, let it burn!' The others looked at each other in surprise, then stood helplessly as the flames spread. Only Mollie saw that split second. The look on Chris's face. It was primeval. It revelled in the fire. There was a glow in his eyes. Then as quickly as it arrived, it vanished. Mollie knew without doubt that Chris's ancestor had burnt the

Manor down. To order or not, it didn't matter. Chris's need to destroy was linked to the burden the men of his family carried. Chris was the last; his burden would die with him. There would be no more of his line. Under control, he turned to her. 'I've been reprieved. Something has been lifted from me…Oh, Moll, I've so much to tell you. And this is Sue.'

So, of course, at that moment, Joanna, Guy and the workers from the estate arrived with trucks and rolled up hosepipes.

'Don't put it out, let it burn!' He ordered again. At which point the flames leapt in the wind to the stable block.

It was too late; the flames too well advanced. They now retreated to the front of the house. The sirens came up the lane. They watched as the team leapt to work, Chris couldn't stop them. But they only had one bowser. The stream on the hill was nearly dry and the main water source was now right in the middle of the flames.

The fire took hold of and burnt through all the buildings. As Mollie watched, she suddenly remembered her laptop and her few possessions. When she asked a firefighter, he shook his head; it was too late to go inside.

Dusk gathered and most people had drifted away. Joanna told Chris and the others to come down to the Manor when it was over. In fact, they were told to leave as the firefighters damped down. They all stood in a group by the cars, not knowing what to say to each other.

'You're will think I'm nuts but cutting my past away has made me freer than I've ever been.' said Chris. 'I've decided what I'm going to do. I'll ask if the estate might like to buy the land back. Then, out of that, we'll totally raze the farm to the ground, so that it seems my family never existed. Then physically and mentally, I'm free.' None of them could find anything to say but understood his logic and agreed.

Mollie saw Sue had her hand in his and suddenly felt more hopeful and happier for Chris than she had ever done.

'Come on, I could do with something stiff to drink after all that!' she said. They set off in the cars and arrived at the Manor where they found Guy and Joanna had prepared the most enormous meal. The beer and wine began to flow. Mollie watched Chris go straight to Joanna and her following look of surprise on her face, but she nodded. Chris would have his happy end.

She found Alan stood beside her. 'I had so much to say to Chris, apologise for sending him off the other week, but now I think I will keep my trap shut as it seems he's going to be okay. Maybe I wasn't meant to say it…that's something to ponder on. If I don't catch up with him directly, you'll give him my love and thank him for finding Steve for me? He's coming to live in one of the cottages for a while and we'll see what happens then.'

Mollie smiled for their happy ending. As Alan turned to talk to Guy about something, Mollie found Ruth behind her, who started a whole conversation on horse therapy and healing. Mollie found it hugely funny as she remembered Sister Jo, but hid her laughter.

The food and wine flowed, and as they sat, the conversation suddenly swung around to Keith and his future.

'I've got the file in the truck!' exclaimed Chris. 'I walked off with it by accident. You can do all the cancellations for me!'

'Lazy bones,' grinned Mollie. 'But seriously, what will happen to him?'

'Well, when you have Chaos gelded, you could have him done too. He then might forget about being a stallion and be a riding horse? I'm sure that half of his trouble is that he's an intelligent creature. Work would keep him occupied,' suggested Joanna.

'I'm not quite at peace with that, so many people leave their horses entire these days. Keith can be a prat, but…it suddenly doesn't seem right, taking something like that away.' Mollie suddenly thought of Chris and caught his eye, but he was grinning at her. 'Any way, why me?'

'I've got the idea that you'll buy him from Diane!' said Joanna.

'I might just do that, but you'll have to break it to her.' Suddenly Mollie was free, too. But only for a split second. 'The lost girls! What will they do?'

'Umm, there's always my place…' said Gary, for the first time ever looking hesitant. Then he seemed to swell up and took a deep breath. 'Of course, as my wife, you would be thoroughly respectable to take them on and I wouldn't have to keep a low profile.' The whole room fell silent as they caught on. 'SO?'

Mollie threw herself at Gary and they all heard a muffled, 'that's a yes then?'

The party became more riotous. Even Ruth wore a glow. When it broke up, they waved goodbye to the Swanage gang, and Mollie piled into Gary's car. The dogs were already asleep in the back, having helped with the leftovers.

Mollie was more than merry. She couldn't put her finger on it. It wasn't this sudden everything coming together. There was another element to it. They drove in quietness. Was this your answer, God? I thought you didn't do big interventions these days. Let me think about this a bit more…

As they passed the farm where a fire engine was there, still damping down, Mollie could see Chaos and Keith playing in the dim light. Keith was cantering slowly around the field and there was something familiar about it. Vaulting! That great big cob from the display. It looked like Keith might have a future after all, even if his breeding days were over. She turned to tell Gary as they drove to her first ever real home.

Further up the hill, nature again took its course. The Shire mare who had a fling with Keith the previous summer gave birth and nursed a palomino colt. Whatever the future held; Keith would live on in this son.

DEAR READER,
THANK YOU!

I hope you have enjoyed Mollie and Chris's adventures! There are lots more books in the Horses and Souls Series. You'll find a taster for the novella, Christmas after all this info!

Please leave a review on Amazon or stars on Goodreads. It means so much to indie authors!

There are many ways to catch up with my books. My blog, Anna's Horse Books, acts like a mailing list. Once a month will come books, interviews, special offers, and much more. There is also an Advent Calendar which will give you loads of ideas for Christmas horse book gifts! On the Homepage, just click on follow by email at the foot of the page or click on the follow widget if you are on Wordpress.

https://booksbyanna619772285.wordpress.com/

You can also join me in my Facebook group for horse book readers! Horse Books for Grown Ups

https://www.facebook.com/

groups/1979909005465261

You can find my Author page on Facebook
https://www.facebook.com/
horsesandogs

Twitter: Anna Rashbrook@AnnaRashbrook

On the next page is a taste of Christmas!

CHRISTMAS

As the festive season begins, the lost girls are up to something. Something horsey, Christmassy and fun. But can they pull it off? Then comes the mystery of the stolen horse…

THE IDEA

'You're not serious?'

'Oh yes, we are!'

Ann looked wearily at the girls over the desk. 'I'm sorry. I'm unable to help. I've got just too much on in the next few weeks. All the weekly groups want a Christmas party. There's the dressage competition, and I'm short staffed. I can't wait for Ruth to arrive and give me a hand. Finding reliable workers is a nightmare.' She pushed her hands through her short black hair, leant back on her chair and looked at them speculatively. 'But. You are welcome to organise it all yourselves. You can use any of the horses, but you have to prepare, groom, set up, clean up, advertise, in fact do it all yourselves and I will only need to come and munch on the great mince pies you'll be giving away…' She grinned with a hint of energy.

'Yaay!' The girls high fived and jumped about.

'What date shall I put in the book, then?'

'The third Saturday in December. We will have broken up on Thursday and we're coming to Mollie's for a few days before we go home for Christmas.' Even Sarah looked enthusiastic.

'And we can have the run of the whole indoor school and yard?'

'Any straw must be cleared from my new surface. You must ask Joanna about parking as there isn't much here. Now that's enough, or I'll be organising it for you. I have a client in ten minutes.'

The girls piled out of the office and talking all at once, walked over to look at the new indoor school. Well, it wasn't a new one, but an old barn moved from the fields to expand the carpark for the Hazeley show. Used for storage, it was ugly; decked in corrugated iron and wood. Much larger than a usual school, it had room for a huge arena and a café and seats that the estate workers had installed. The girls looked around in awe, no more freezing if they wanted lessons in the winter. The new sound system meant they had the perfect place for their vaulting team. They piled into the café area, bought sweets and drinks from the machine, and settled down for a planning meeting.

'I still think we should tell Mollie about this. I don't understand how you translate this into a surprise/thank you/wedding present for her?' Sarah had to have the first word.

'We did all agree that this is the kind of Christmas present she'd appreciate.' Debbie glared back.

'OY!' stepped in Jenny, for once asserting herself. 'If we can't agree at this stage, we're doomed to failure. Take it as settled, Sarah, and let's crack on.'

Printed in Great Britain
by Amazon